The Way We Live

# THE WAY WE LIVE:
# STORIES BY UTAH WOMEN

Edited by
*Ellen Fagg*

Signature Books • Salt Lake City
1994

*"In the Shadows of Upshot-Knothole" first appeared in* A Brief History of Male Nudes in America, *by Dianne Nelson, published by University of Georgia Press, 1993; reprinted by permission of the author and University of Georgia Press.*

Cover design by Ron Stucki
Cover photo by Rosalind Newmark

∞ *The Way We Live* was printed on acid-free paper and meets the permanence of paper requirements of the American National Standard for Information Sciences. This book was composed, printed, and bound in the United States.

97   96   95   94      5   4   3   2   1

Library of Congress Cataloging-in-Publication Data
The way we live : stories by Utah women / edited by Ellen Fagg.
         p.    cm.
    ISBN 1-56085-062-0
    1. Short stories, American—Utah.    2. Short stories, American—
Women authors.    3. Utah—Social life and customs—Fiction.
4. Women—Utah—Fiction.    I. Fagg, Ellen.
PS571.U8W39    1994
813'.01089287—dc20                                        94-38215
                                                                    CIP

# contents

# AMAZING PLACE

My mother lives in Oregon, but her name is already carved into a headstone, my father's, in Salt Lake City. For six years I've made an annual pilgrimage to his grave at Wasatch Lawn. These are my rituals: I plant American flags in the grass in front of the granite marker. I balance pots of purple and yellow mums upright. I carefully arrange cut flowers to cover my mother's name and date of her birth, in case I decide to send her a picture.

This year on Memorial Day, the afternoon sun is so hot that I worry it will bleach the blue sky out of the photo. As I wedge the flower pots into the grass, I hear warbling, reedy notes. I see a bagpiper to the north. I whistle the piper's tune over and over again before I recognize what it is: *Amazing Grace*.

I shouldn't be, but somehow I feel connected to this place. I was raised on a filbert orchard two states west of Utah, but I've worked in my father's hometown, Salt Lake City, for most of my adult life. When I think about what writers refer to as *place*, I remember my pioneer ancestors who saw the Great Salt Lake Basin as the promised land, and I remember where my father's body finally settled.

In Utah, family ties pull with the force of gravity. My father certainly felt that tug. He was raised here, then left to fly a P-38 in the Philippines. After he returned home from World War II, he married my mother. Together they raised our family on an Oregon farm, near where my mother still lives, my brothers and sisters close by. My father left Utah, told getaway stories, but when it came time to be buried, he came home, a Utah body.

Sweat pools behind my knees as I crouch here by his grave, located four rows north of his younger sister, five plots west of his older brother. There's ground here reserved for my mother. I rub the space on the stone that will be engraved with the date of her death. I think of all the decisions my mother didn't get to make, all the stories they didn't pass down. This was my father's place, not hers; my mother never claimed Utah as her home but my father died first.

Our western myths are based on the stories of men, men like my father's, who scouted and hunted and farmed in the shadow of the everlasting hills. They were rugged settlers who transformed a cheatgrass desert on the shores of a salty sea into Zion; men who built one version, at least, of paradise.

The short fictions in this collection add something else: the narrative voices of fast-talking contemporary women who aren't content to settle on a man's frontier, who are staking out claims to the emotional landscape. Stories like these twelve—from women writers, most of whom live in the New West—are helping to reinvent the history of men and women whose lives collide under a big sky. These writers write about suffering in the promised land, and why a woman might stay. Or leave.

As a reader, I started looking for a collection like this several years ago. I was hungry to read stories that unveiled more narratives of the West, stories tracing connections of the heart.

Some of the writers whose stories are included in this book have published nationally; many have earned graduate degrees in writing programs, notably at the University of Utah; others are just starting to win awards and publish in literary journals. All of these writers are somehow rooted in Utah. All deserve to be discovered.

What is revealed here isn't religion, although the culture of Utah's saints cuts through these stories like irrigation canals in the desert. These are stories from Mormon country, where horses are named Adversity and Zion and polygamists live on raspberry fields by the shores of Bear Lake.

These are getaway stories, gambling tales. Audrey, a woman stranded in "Nevada Border Towns," bets on her grandmother's advice: "Love is only a decision to stop moving." In "Sisterwives: The Order Things Took," a child bride wears an eggshell cream dress decorated with a fringe of colored ribbons. "Pure white," Evie says, "makes we women look too dangerous for words."

A younger, even more precocious child talks. She talks about the time she and her mother deserted their movie-star wannabe father. She talks about the bombs exploding above their southern Utah ranch. "I was a year old," says the child narrator of "In the Shadows of Up-shot-Knothole," "just a small flowing river of sounds, words that spun unrecognizable, but my mother and I had complete conversations anyway. She says that she had been waiting her whole life for me. When I arrived, there was a lot for us to talk about."

If "literature is mostly about having sex and not having children," as critic David Lodge writes, "and life is the other way around," then these stories are from a land where people are in labor—literally. A childless woman follows pregnant strangers to offer her services as a birth coach in "Where Detail in the Background Is Permissible." There's the mother in "Mouth to Mouth" who labors under fear, the fear of high places and the fear of loving her children.

This is rugged emotional country, filled with characters like Del, who stands out from the minute he races into town, according to Dawna, owner of the local bar who explains "Why I Left Paradise." "It was true the car looked silly in this kind of place, against the dust and the wide sky, and so did his new boots and his white felt hat still clean from the box," she says. "'What'll you have?' I said. And he smiled, and I said, 'Don't be too sure.'"

Dawna's story unfolds the heat of combustible sex, while the bragging-rights kind of intercourse unravels a hard secret in "Blue, Blue, My Love is Blue." These are stories from love's combat zone, tales of shifting, heart-breaking emotion, inspiration provided by a singer with rolling kneecaps and "crazy hoppin' rollin' legs" in "Some Body Parts Remember a War." There are other body parts, too, pressed skin-to-skin in "Finding a Wife for My Brother." In addition to all the connections, there's the long distance separating two emotionally isolated women in "Calla Lilies."

Here also are sketches of the complicated, treacherous territory dividing mothers and daughters. "My mother was six-foot-one and a natural platinum blonde and I was dark and short and stocky," says Mim Jr. in "The Way I Live," "so obviously I must have taken after my father, whoever he may have been, which is what I say when I want to make Mim really mad."

Julie, the narrator of "Waltzing the Cat," recalls seeing photos of a time when her parents looked like two people who could actually have sex with each other. "Everything was perfect with your father and me before you were born," her mother tells her, confusion in her voice, but not blame. "I guess he was jealous, or something, and then all the best parts of him just went away.

But," she adds, as she makes the cat a plate of sour cream herring, chopped up fine, "it has all been worth it because of you."

*Because of you.* Stories about the view beyond the next canyon, about gambling on a heartbeat, about the strong gravital pull of love and family and landscape. These are weighty stories as powerful as the myths of paradise, stories about the wildness that remains in this amazing place.

Ellen Fagg
Salt Lake City
September 1994

# one

# WHY I LEFT PARADISE

*Katharine Coles*

It wasn't long after Harris started carrying his pistol into the Bucket that Ed Jakes the sheriff and Tommy Belew the mayor got together at the cafe to talk about an ordinance to stop him—it was easier somehow than talking sense to him about Dimmer—and it was hardly any time after that before the men from the NRA started showing up in Paradise and talking about winning the west and freedom and the wild frontier and all that history, some of which still seemed pretty modern-day to us and some of which we had done our darnedest to forget. True, I walked out as far into the desert as I could every day just to be alone under the sky, but if anything, that was what made people around here talk, and it had nothing to do with what the NRA boys were saying as far as I could see.

Not, like I pointed out to Tommy and Ed later in the

1

bar when they came in to tell me about it, that boys hadn't been carrying guns in their trucks or even into the Bucket for years and nobody minded. But those were hunting rifles or working guns with no clear malicious intent attached to them.

And not that there hadn't even been a few shootings around town, when things got a little wilder than usual, but they took place rarely and privately, in people's houses or trailers or out in the desert among the sage, and everyone could say afterward they might have predicted them—unlike in the city, where we all knew, from the news, people got shot in grocery stores or out on the sidewalks in front of their houses.

But Harris, he bought his pistol with a purpose and everyone knew it, and he walked into the bar every night with the gun strapped around his hip for us all to see, and then he'd start drinking and looking around him. I can't say, though I must have loved him at the time, that it was good for business. When Harris started talking loud and looking at people with his hand on his hip above the holster, customers started picking up their hats, and who can blame them?

Of course, after the NRA boys came the gun control people followed, and then the reporters, and this changed everything. Like Tommy said, none of them had any real business here, but all of a sudden there was more work in the Bucket than I could handle alone, and I hired on a couple of town girls as barmaids whose husbands would let them wear their blouses unbuttoned one or two.

Walking in there at night I would hardly know the old place, filled with men in suits or brand new cowboy boots, half of them with holsters on their hips or strapped across their shoulders, the other half mostly in beards. It was like the movies, only more so. Nobody who saw it on the drive-in screen over in Rock Springs would have believed it.

As far as I could tell, the NRA boys thought the show of guns made their drinking less recreational, more a serious demonstration of liberty at work; and the gun control guys mostly sat around looking sad and peaceful, except when one got in it with an NRA boy and they started squaring off over a pool table, hitting one ball into another with serious intent, holding their cues like weapons.

Even then, I kept wanting to say to them, "We could have handled it ourselves." After all, I thought at the time, it wasn't them we cared about, just Harris, who was a little funny and who had his reasons that we all knew and, more than strangers anyway, understood.

But then looking them all over I didn't know anymore. For us, most of them were too skinny or too soft, and within a couple of days they all had new sunburns and were walking around bowlegged like they'd been galloping around Wyoming on horses all their lives.

Nobody was fooled. In fact, it wasn't even until Del showed up late in the game that Harris developed his conspiracy idea into anything more than one of his dim notions, and things began to get serious.

It all started the first time Dimmer burned down Harris's trailer.

That time, Harris just stood there in the hot, wavering light from the flames, his arms crossed over his chest and the bottle of Dickel he'd brought home to help him and me ease into morning, and laughed. There was no conspiracy yet; Harris had plenty of insurance for once and admitted he didn't have much he minded losing beyond a snug place to take me to when we got tired of looking at my little house, or even to go home alone to when we got tired of looking at each other.

And once can be an accident.

At any rate, somehow Harris never even thought of Dimmer. Looking into the embers, he dropped his arm around me and kissed me and said, "You don't mind if I don't bring over my silk pajamas, do you?"

Some people who hadn't been around Paradise long and remembered the mattress in the jail, and even Henry from the State Farm office in Rock Springs, wondered for awhile that time if Harris hadn't had something to do with the fire himself, but after not very long Henry admitted there were too many of us willing to swear Harris had been glued to that barstool all night. The flames were shooting high already by the time we all came out from the bar into the street to see, so the case was settled pretty quick as those things go. And nobody said anything about Dimmer, who had just stood and watched the trailer burn like the rest of us, but with maybe a more devoted attention, until his mother came and took him home.

The second time, there was no question in any of our minds about Dimmer, and still nobody said a word, least of all to Henry.

Harris was working on an oil rig miles out of town, and he didn't even get back until the trailer was just a pile of charred metal and singed plastic and linoleum. I got there with the rest of the crowd that poured out on Main Street as the smoke rose and word spread. Dimmer was there before us, and nobody had seen him arrive. As I watched the flames, I could feel him standing just behind me, too close. I could smell him, that sweet smell I remembered from junior high. When the fire was just past its height, Dimmer's mother as always elbowed her way through the crowd and grabbed him by the hand, and though he was my age and a head taller he followed her home like a child.

I watched until the flames died then went home and got my sweater and a magazine and went back to wait for Harris. Once I looked down the block and saw Dimmer standing there watching me, but when I raised my hand he turned and walked away. Then Harris pulled up in his truck. I know he saw me sitting on the curb but it was a long time before he reached over and opened the passenger door.

"So," he said, "tell me."

"Everyone came out to watch. You could see the smoke all over town."

"I should have expected it," he said, "but a man never does."

I knew he'd caught on about Dimmer. "It's always been this way," I said. "It isn't personal."

He looked over at me for a second, then said, "The hell it isn't," and got back in the truck and started it up, and we drove over to Mason Clark's who owns the Paradise Hardware and got him up away from his supper to unlock the shop. Then Harris stood over the gun case and weighed each gun in his hand, not neglecting even the dainty pearl-handled ones for women, and finally after pulling back the hammers and looking solemnly down the chambers of a couple of blue, sleek looking pistols chose the gun he wanted and signed over his weekly paycheck.

As soon as I saw what he was after, I started meaning to say something, just waiting for the right moment, a moment of air or light; but that time never came.

Finally, I said to him, "It was just Dimmer."

And Harris said, "And his same lighter he used on the old school and the hospital and even, if you recall, the

Bucket once. One of these days, he'll torch the whole damn town for love."

I said, "The Bucket is right next to the fire station."

But Harris hadn't always lived in Paradise, and besides he needed something bigger in his life. And I have to admit, looking at him so serious over those guns, I wanted to take him home. So he took to packing that pistol right there on his hip where we could all see it and start to worry sometime around his second or third drink.

I was working a couple of lunches a week at the cafe then to help pay off the mortgage on the bar, and nights there at the Bucket where Harris did most of his drinking and where I'd been pulling beer since Daddy got too sick to stand up behind the taps. It had been tight, but I was just beginning to see the light, just starting to breathe easy. When Daddy died, people told me to sell and move to Salt Lake or Cheyenne at least and maybe get a job in an office, the bar was no place for a girl barely twenty, but I knew by then I loved it all: the warped-and-flecked mirrors; the larger-than-life painting of an old saloon singer whose name was long forgotten but who reclined still, fleshy and glorious, on the wall; the dark, splintering wood and the sawdust on the floors.

Over the years, though Mama had wanted to paint over the singer with white paint, Daddy had tried to touch her up as her skin peeled away or dimmed with age or where the smoke from the fire darkened her, and her nipples were vivid and too new looking even under the low lights. People were right, the place was falling apart, but finally it was about to be mine.

Those days, if Harris wasn't at his trailer when the sun came up people knew they could find him at my house, and that's where he stayed both times after the fires while he waited for the checks from State Farm. And the first time, I have to admit, it was a little like a vacation, with Harris counting on my toes at night the little things he was going to buy me with what was left over from the insurance—a white floating nightgown, rhinestone barrettes for my hair—then working his way from my feet toward a kiss in which his upward progress involved our whole bodies.

Of course, there was no money left over from the insurance. I could have told him there wouldn't be—there hadn't been even enough from the time the bar flooded or the time it burned—but I was as close to loving Harris during those weeks when he was spending in his mind as I ever had been, and he was happy so I let him be. Both times he got just enough to buy a trailer even more beat than the one before—after, of course, he had already dropped a couple hundred on celebrating his anticipations.

The interior of the last trailer glowed with a kind of green, underwatery light, and it was infused with a smell that I could never quite identify, though it reminded me of the apartment over the bar just before Daddy died—sort of medicinal and decayed at the same time. And try as he might, grading the ground over, crawling around underneath looking at wheels and suspensions, Harris never could get that trailer level.

Everything that happened in there happened askew: the one time we shared the narrow bed, I slept next to the wall and felt his weight against me all night long, my shoulder wedged against plastic wood-grain paneling; and when I cooked a dinner in his oven, the casseroles and pie fillings all slid over to the north side of the pans and stuck that way, so the full table was a dizzying field of slopes. More and more, Harris was waking up in my level white bedroom and pouring out his morning coffee at my solid kitchen table.

What was wrong with Dimmer nobody really knew, though it had always been wrong, and when he was a year old or so, I'd been told, and his mother had seen enough other babies to know something was the matter, she took him down every few weeks for awhile to Salt Lake and the children's hospital to try to find out what could be done. When the doctors told her to give up, she did.

And Paradise just took him in like we'd always taken in the odd ones from among us, with even a certain kind of love no more cruel, maybe even a little gentler, than the love we gave to those strong and close to our hearts.

He was a fixture we took for granted in the elementary school, his desk always behind mine because of the alphabet. When we started taking the bus out to the junior high, Dimmer took to sitting in the seat behind me there, too, as if only a view of the back of my head kept him located.

Mostly, I paid no attention to him, but once, some of the older girls started laughing at him—asking him to flick his Bic for them, to light their fires, as if he would have any idea at all what they were talking about—and he looked so lost with his fists shoved down in his pockets I said, "Leave him alone."

He just looked at me then moved up real close but not quite touching. His white T-shirt and jeans were filthy, but I caught for the first time then that sweet smell I knew was exactly the smell of his skin. After that nobody said a word to him when I was there. I got used to seeing him almost everywhere I went.

Dimmer started small, I know, with little child's fires made of twigs and leaves. Then, the fires started to spread, taking bushes and finally whole vacant lots. Once he lit the papers in his mother's bedroom wastebasket; the plastic melted and began to burn the carpet before his mother smelled the smoke and pulled the garden hose, water running all the way, in at the kitchen door, through the dining room and living room, and up the stairs.

And once on the Fourth of July he and another boy,

Buddy Werner, found a pint of vodka still a quarter full behind the Bucket. Any other boy would have drunk it down, as Buddy wanted to, but Dimmer lit five sparklers, dropped them in, and screwed the lid back on. We heard the explosion in the bar. It didn't sound dangerous, more like a muffled loss of air, but Buddy's screams brought us out.

Daddy bound up Buddy's thigh, sliced through to the bone, with bar towels, then loaded him into the truck to drive him to the clinic. I gave Dimmer the hose and he sprayed the blood and bubbled, fractured glass down the asphalt in first a red and then a widening pink fan, keeping the hose on it like I told him until the water ran clear.

The time he lit up the trashcans behind the Bucket on a Saturday night, I was fourteen and just coming down from the apartment over the bar where Daddy and I lived to ask permission for something, I don't remember what. I remember I was wearing a new dress made from a pattern I saw in *Seventeen*, with a skirt that would billow out when I swished it just right, and so I held on to the doorframe with one hand and swung around it into the bar, and first my skirt and then I came right up against Harris, new in town then to work on the oil rigs. I'd never seen him before.

He stepped back and took me by my elbows and looked at me for a minute. Then a flash right over his shoulder caught my eye and I looked up in time to see the back wall of the bar give way to a sheet of fire.

Like the rest of them, on his very first evening after
rolling into town in that little white sportscar Harris
looked at and called a toy right off, Del was in at the
Bucket letting us all take a look at him. It was true the car
looked silly in this kind of space, against the dust and
wide sky, and so did his new boots and the white felt hat
still clean from the box, but he wasn't carrying a gun that
I could see, and I could see too first thing that though he
was handsome in that young sort of way—smooth-faced
and blond—he wasn't too sweet or too stupid either.

I was leaning over the bar talking to Harris and letting
him look down my blouse when Del walked in. I straight-
ened up and raised my eyebrows at Harris, not in an
appreciative kind of way I thought but more like I was
curious, and gave Del a minute to find a free table and
settle in before I walked over.

Del looked me up and down and said, "Now, you
couldn't be anybody but Dawna." I had my picture in the
front window with my name under it the way Daddy
always had so it couldn't have been that tough to know,
but at the time his words seemed like a casual kind of
miracle.

"What'll you have?" I said. And he smiled, and I said,
"Don't be so sure," but then I heard the door shut even
through the noise from the crowd and when I turned
around Harris was gone. So it wasn't that hard after all to

sit down and take a break with Del, or to walk outside with him and let him kiss me and run his hands up inside my blouse while over his shoulder the bug zapper sizzled the mosquitoes, or to take him home with me after closing and give him a drink while I showered the smell of cigarettes out of my hair, or to walk back into the living room and sit down on his lap wearing only my satin charmeuse kimono I'd ordered from the back pages of *Cosmo*.

The next night in the Bucket, Harris was carrying his gun. Not wearing it like he'd taken to doing anyway, but carrying it in his hand when he walked through the door, and I could see he'd already had a few. I raised my eyebrows at Del where he was sitting over in the corner and shook my head to let him know I couldn't walk by his table for now.

Harris came on over to the bar and I brought him a shot of Dickel and then another and then the bottle, all without us passing a word. Finally, about half through the fifth, he crooked his finger at me and I went over. Leaning over the bar toward me, he pointed the gun behind him at Del, pointed that gun with his finger on the trigger, and said, "He's part of it."

Slowly, the bar quieted down. Men opened their coats and moved their hands to their hips or hearts.

I said, "Put that down." Then, "I don't know what you mean."

"I couldn't shoot a kid like Dimmer," he said, like he was asking me for something.

It had never crossed my mind a man might start firing for lack of something real to shoot at. I said, "Del's not in your way. This is something else."

He said, "It can only get worse. Don't let yourself get taken in."

I said, "Maybe you'd better find yourself another place to drink."

I could see reporters pulling out little notebooks and starting to write. Somebody shouted, "Smile, Dawna," and a camera flashed.

I said, "Fuck off." Then, to Harris, "You too. I wasn't born yesterday."

He leaned way over toward me, I think mostly to keep from falling, and set down the gun on the bar and grabbed both my elbows kind of rough. "You were, Dawna," he said, and looked into my eyes. "Remember what I said. But do what you have to."

I said, "I always do."

He kept looking at me like that and pushing my elbows down into the wood of the bar. And suddenly Del was there putting one hand down on the back of Harris's neck and the other down on the gun next to us and saying, "Would you mind letting go of the lady's arms?"

The camera flashed again, and when Harris let go Del thanked him and handed him his gun and asked me if he could buy me a drink on my break.

Then Ed pushed in shouting through the crowd and we all ran outside and down to the motel. Del's little convertible was pulled up in front of the door to his room, number 4. Its seats hadn't even caught. The vinyl looked a little melted, was all, and the newspaper that had been piled up in them and set alight blew in weightless, vivid shreds up and over our heads into the desert.

All that August, Del wouldn't tell me whose side he was on. I'd quit at the cafe since the bar business was so good, and in the mornings when there weren't meetings or hearings Del would go back to the motel and make phone calls on his credit card, or he'd sit at my kitchen table with his little computer on his lap and type out letters for the afternoon mail while I walked out the back door and over the dry earth toward the horizon.

Once I walked out to Harris's trailer—he was out at the fields—and let myself in with my key and sat down at the table in the green light. There was a little screw on the floor and I picked it up and set it down on the table's slanted surface and let it roll, then did it again and thought what I knew about Del.

I couldn't have wanted to know much. Looking back, I don't even remember what made me realize about the wife, but however that news came—whether I looked down at an address or overheard something, or, as it even seems possible, he told me sometime that first night or week—it didn't make so much difference that I stopped letting him come home with me at night. It wasn't even that I was so taken with him, though there was a lot of charm there; it was more like I knew from the start that all I wanted from him was a taste of something I'd only read about in my magazines.

It seemed like Harris knew it, too; after that night in the bar, he stayed completely away.

Before I left the trailer I found an old envelope and a pen. "I was here," I wrote on the back. "Love, Dawna."

Here's the difference: Harris was a body made solid by work but soft around the middle by love and beer and the kind of food that sticks to you. When he came in from the oil fields he had a shine around him and the smell of dirt and oil and the sun and sweat both from the day and the night; sometimes, kissing him on his way to the shower, I would think I could smell myself on him left over from the night before, a dark smell not quite erased by the day's heat and motion. I'd leave for work as he came in, and later he'd come into the bar smelling like soap, his hair combed back wet. At night, he would take off his shirt and Wranglers and Fruit-of-the-Looms and drop them by the bed and crawl in next to me already ready. In the morning, he picked up the clothes from the floor and put them back on and pulled his cap on over his hair. He filled his thermos and came back into the bedroom to kiss me goodbye and then he left for the oil fields just as the sun was rising, and I went back to sleep up for the bar shift or I got up when he was gone and packed a lunch and a magazine and headed out into the desert.

So when Del woke me in full sun that first morning with his fingers on my mouth like something out of the movies, I sat up and said, "What's wrong?" but when he kissed me I lay right back down. He still smelled of a spicy cologne. His limbs and body were harder than Harris's, but at first I was disappointed by what seemed a lack of substance. Even his skin felt too smooth to be quite real—running my hands over his back I remembered Harris's moles and scaly spots and odd wild hairs and marveled. And Del's limbs were like wires twisted together tight. Already that morning I could tell he was stronger than I thought.

After awhile he pulled me up and into the shower and washed my hair and back and then I did his.

He said, "Do you read all those magazines?" and "What are you doing here?" and I said, "This is where I live." He stayed with me until I told him I needed to rest before work, but he was back in time to walk me over to the bar. It was still hot, and we walked slow.

"My mother wanted to call me Aurora," I said. He had his hand laid across my shoulders, but I wasn't sweating there. And when we were strolling past Millie's with the white beaded cardigan in the window and I stopped to look as always, he went right inside and bought it even though I told him not to.

"It's just right," he said, and I said, "What will people say?" but when he held it for me I slid my arms in.

It was a kind of game at first. I would say, "What are you doing here?"

He would say, "I heard this was where I'd find you."

When we stopped making love every time he said that, he started to say, "I like to be where things happen."

Nobody else knew either. On the street, Ed Jakes the sheriff or Tommy Belew the mayor or even in the end men I didn't know would stop me and say, "What's Del's part?" and I would just smile and walk on.

To tease him, I would say, "Harris says it's all part of a conspiracy."

He would say, "Harris is smarter than he looks," or "Harris is just the bone the dogs are worrying."

And I would say no and tell him about the time just after the Bucket fire when Harris got all lit up on bourbon and wrote me a note and tied it around the shaft of an arrow and shot that arrow right through my bedroom window at four a.m. I opened my eyes to see it quivering in the wall above my bed, the fragments of glass glimmering on the floor under the window.

The note said, "You looked so innocent. I want to touch you so much it makes me shake."

First thing the next day, Daddy said, "You're still a

child, this is no place for you, he could have killed you," and sat down and wrote away to Grandma back East where Mama had lived before Daddy met her.

Or I'd tell Del about the time Ed Jakes had put Harris in jail just to sober him up one night and the next morning found him curled up in one corner sleeping on the floor, the sheets and mattress on the iron bed burned to cinders. "Only Harris," I said.

"Or someone just like him," Del said.

"Everyone else is harmless," I said. "And so is he."

"In the abstract," he said.

"So what do you think?"

"I think there'll be a lot of fuss, then everyone will leave and the town will be just like it was but a lot emptier and either richer or poorer by comparison, depending on who you are, and Harris will carry his gun until he gets tired of it, maybe never."

He was right. The ordinance was defeated; the reporters did a whole lot of last-minute interviews and took pictures of people on horseback or standing by pickup trucks or holding up their hunting rifles victoriously. Ed Belew was on the front page of a big paper back East: the photo shows him standing in the doorway of the Bucket, his great-grandpa's holster and pistol buckled around his waist. Somewhere around are shots of me in tight jeans with the desert behind me; the photographer said he wanted to shoot me naked, he'd make me famous, but I said he didn't know and anyway, enough was enough.

As far as I can remember nobody bothered to take a picture of Harris. The NRA boys spent a couple of days drinking the Bucket dry, then they packed up their rental cars and drove off down to the big airport in Salt Lake with the gun control guys and then the reporters hot on their heels.

And the next noon I hung up a "Closed for the Night" sign on the Bucket and Del and I walked out my back yard and into the desert, west, with the sun right overhead.

"Watch out for rattlesnakes," I said. I carried the blanket and he carried the basket with sandwiches and apples and a bottle of bourbon. We climbed the stile over the fence onto Mason's ranch—Del went first and turned to take my hand as I came over—and made our way through the sagebrush down to the swimming hole.

It seems now like that was the last really hot day of the summer, the last day when the heat feels like it's pushing you right down into the ground while you walk. By the time we got to the creek, our legs were covered with dust and I could see the sweat curling down over the sunburn already peeling on his back.

"There's a lot of poison out here," he said, and I said, "It's everywhere. Here, you just know where it is."

"What more could you want?" he said.

We spread out the blanket and took off our clothes and teetered over the sharp rocks into the water. We paddled and pushed each other under and he touched me where the cold had tightened up my flesh. Then, still naked, we ate our lunch on the bank and drank out of the bottle, then we swam again and then he pulled me back out onto the blanket and started to kiss me in earnest.

Once, he pulled away and said, "Do you ever think of leaving?" but I couldn't tell why he was asking so I didn't answer but put my hands behind his neck, and he went right back down to my mouth.

I had shut my eyes and was feeling my way into his touch, letting it travel down below the surface of my skin, when I felt the shadow. It was another second before I remembered I had seen no clouds anywhere and opened my eyes. The sun was behind him; at first I thought it was Harris, but the shape was too tall and too slight. His hands were in his pockets and his shoulders hunched; he was standing very still.

"Dimmer," I said, "go home." And he took one hand from his pocket and reached it out toward me and just stood there. Del had rolled aside and after a minute I got up and picked my way barefoot through the sand and put my hand in Dimmer's. I could feel Del's sweat evaporating off me. Dimmer kept his eyes on mine but I could tell he was seeing everything he wanted to.

"Go home," I said, and he held my hand for a second then dropped it and turned and walked away.

It was dark when we got back; I showered and put the steaks on while Del showered and then we ate, silent, looking at each other over the bowl of Minute Rice and the casseroled vegetables and the salad. He hadn't said anything but of course I knew he would leave the next day or the day after, it didn't much matter. I looked past him at the window, but it was dark and I could see only my own kitchen distorted in the glass.

"Did you get what you wanted?" I said.

He just looked at me.

I said, "For a long time, I thought there was nothing here. I would look at my magazines and imagine the big cities, each with some pulse traveling through it that I wanted to feel. But that summer Daddy sent me away to Grandma, I would dream I was standing on a hill in the middle of the city and the buildings were in rubble around me. Finally, I could see as far as I needed to, and then the ruins were gone and I was walking out in the open desert."

"Could I come back?" he said.

"Call first," I said.

Something moved in the window—it was neither of us, and I got up and went and opened the back door.

Harris stood there, his hand on his gun. "I think you'd better come," he said.

Even before we got around to the front of the house, I could see where the sky was lit up over Main Street and flickering. The couple of blocks of businesses were going up on the west side of the street; fires had been set at either end, and they were moving fast toward the center, toward the fire station and the Bucket and Millie's.

The buildings were mostly old wood that had dried out for decades there under the sun. Every man in town was out. They'd opened the hydrant in front of the station, and Tommy trained a hose on the roofs of the unburned buildings there, leaning back against the force of the water.

"He got the trailer, too," Harris said.

We stood for a minute, Harris and then me and then Del. Del had grabbed my sweater. They each had one of my hands; they both stood close, their shoulders touching mine. Then I shook off their hands and dug my keys out of my jeans and walked under the arch of water from the hose and unlocked the door of the Bucket and went in.

Later, people would say I was in shock; some would say it was grief still about Daddy, but having sat over him so many nights I knew how to let him go when the time came. They would say I should have got married to Harris and settled down long ago if I was going to stay in Paradise; like the other women behind their lace curtains ordered in from Sears I should have done the dishes from the night before and hung the wash out on the line and stood a minute to chat over the fence instead of keeping the bar 'til late then walking out of town alone in the mornings.

I went behind the bar and pulled out a bottle of

bourbon and a glass and then grabbed a handful of quarters out of the cash register and dropped them into the jukebox and pushed the numbers for all the mournful songs—Patsy Cline and Hank Williams and Tammy Wynette. Behind the music I could hear the low roar of fire all around. Then I sat down and started to drink, not too fast but steady, and when I looked up Harris was putting down his own empty glass on the table and reaching for the bottle.

"I promised I'd bring you out," he said.

I said, "The fire will never get here."

"Then come on." He reached down and pulled me up by the hand, but instead of leading me outside he put his arms around me and started to dance me between the tables. He was bigger than I remembered, solid and nourished and starting to get tired in the general way. I felt like I was floating; I didn't have to move because he moved me the way he wanted me to go, and my body went. He put his hand behind my head and pressed it to his chest. I could smell the sweat and feel the pulse in my ear, either his or mine, and under my left elbow I felt the handle of the gun.

"Why didn't you shoot him?" I said.

"I told you," he said. Then, "It was always for you." He laid his cheek down on the top of my head and sang along with Freddy Fender—"If he brings you happiness, I wish you all the best"—in the same trembling warble.

"I know," I said. And then the song finished and we

danced the next one and went back to the table for the one after, but before he sat down he unbuckled the holster and laid it next to the bottle. Neither of us said anything for a minute. Then I got up and put a quarter in the pool table and started to rack the balls, lazy. I picked up the two-ball and hefted it in my hand like I was going to throw it, first at Harris, who kept grinning, and then at the old mirror over the bar.

In the mirror's cloudy, wavering surface I could just see the tops of our heads down to our eyebrows, and above them the reflected painting, the lush old-time whore stretched out around her brilliant nipples, one gartered leg crossed demurely over the other, her toes still dark with smoke from the last fire.

I aimed at the higher nipple and held the ball for a long time at my shoulder, then wound up and threw. A wave rippled the whole glass; the cracks spread through it and it fell in a shattered sheet of light to the floor.

I let out my breath and sat down at the table. We looked at each other and started to laugh; I threw back my head and Harris laid his down on the table. His shoulders shook; he started to pound the table with the palms of his hands. I brought my head forward again and looked straight in front of me where the glass stood out in a jagged edge around where the mirror had been; I was still laughing, the tears running down my cheeks. We were pulling deep as we could for breath in the thick, hazy air and howling.

Then I unsnapped the holster and pulled out the gun. He didn't stop me, just watched with a smile on his face like he had seen it coming, though I knew I hadn't. I ran my hand down the barrel, smooth and oddly warm.

"It's heavy," I said. I still couldn't breathe. I had fired a rifle once, when I was a kid, just at some tin cans on the back fence. I remembered the way it had kicked against my shoulder—I'd had a bruise there afterward for days.

My eyes burned. The static from the fire had grown louder but the jukebox had stopped. I knew I had put in more quarters than that. I put the heel of my hand against my chest where my breath was burning me.

He would come in for me, I knew. I could almost feel him standing next to me, could smell that sweet smell. I held the gun and sighted and waited for the door to open, for Dimmer to appear and hold out his hand through the smoke.

# two

# IN THE SHADOWS OF UPSHOT-KNOTHOLE

*Dianne Nelson*

My mother and I ran away only one time, on a sunny May morning when the world was about to end. She didn't know where we were running to, but my mother, Lorraine, was smart and she would have figured something out, a place for us to go—Cedar City or Tonopah. For a while after she met my father and married him, she said that she only thought between her legs, but time had passed and I'd come along and life had resumed its normal colors and my mother was trying to think with her head again. Lewis and Elly Barlow, our nearest neighbors, lived almost four miles away on a dirt road that cut through sagebrush and scruffy cedar, and since my mother was on foot and I was in a stroller, their house was the first stop on our way to somewhere, to any place without movie stars.

We had left my father back at the house sitting sullenly on a kitchen chair, and even then he looked a little too much like Tony Curtis to my mother's way of thinking. Black slick hair, a face that you remembered as cheekbones and clear eyes. He was all shoulders and tight waist and he had a raw, sleepy sexiness that he knew nothing about. That morning, though, his arms were folded over his chest and he sat in the chair tipped back on its two legs and he was staring at the wall, tired and angry. He said my mother didn't understand him.

The breakfast dishes had just been washed—cups and bowls and plates stacked into the small artful piles that women can make of ordinary things. My mother had dried her hands, stepped over me on the floor where I had balled the rug up around me, and gone to my father's side. "This is what I understand," she said, her voice rising, straining, finally sending Lowry, our big near-sighted collie, slinking from the room. "You'd rather go off and play than stay here with your wife and daughter."

My father had no response to that—sometimes he was tongue tied; sometimes he needed to filter things and kick some dirt before clarity rushed him—but it didn't matter because my mother spun around, walked back to the bedroom and began to collect the odds-and-ends that would compose our survival kit: a hairbrush, a silver baby spoon, a Sears and Roebuck catalog, talcum powder, an eyebrow pencil, diapers. She threw them into a water-stained overnight case and she did it loudly so that my father could hear in the next room, but he didn't budge. They were at one of those impasses where husbands and wives sometimes find themselves—exhausted, speechless, the reckless fear that things will never be the same growing larger and more distinct by the second.

My mother didn't say good-bye. She just walked out into the kitchen with me on her hip and we stood there like a last photograph for my father. He never looked away from the green-and-white wallpaper checks on the kitchen wall. I drooled and gurgled and reached for him, my mother tells me, my hands round and fat as little pin cushions, but he didn't move. He had a point to make and he was serious about it, the chair tipped back, his silence stretching beyond the movies, beyond all the dark-haired leading men into our early morning reality.

My mother was in every way his match. She gathered our things like the slender tornado she could be. Gracefully she walked down the front steps of the house with all the future she could carry—me and an overloaded suitcase and a wobbly baby stroller—and when we were out in the yard, she put the suitcase down, wrestled the stroller with one hand, locked the legs into place, and slipped me in.

I was a year old, just a small flowing river of sounds, words that spun unrecognizable, but my mother and I had complete conversations anyway. She says that she had been waiting her whole life for me. When I arrived, there was a lot for us to talk about.

With the suitcase in one hand and the stroller handle in the other, she pushed and explained. "Everything is going to be all right, sweetheart. These things just happen. Your dad has some silly idea stuck in his head and he can't get rid of it."

I reached up with one hand and batted the endless blue sky and jabbered a hundred things back to my mother, and she listened and sorted it out and understood.

"I know. I know," she said. "He's immature. More looks than brains."

I took hold of the plastic stroller tray in front of me and shook it and it seemed to be just the advice my mother was looking for.

"You're right," she said. "I've gone weak and one-minded every time he turned those big blues on me. Putty in his hands. But no more. It's time to get things rolling." As if it were a pact we were keeping, she stopped and reached down and touched my head—a mass of curls that kept me prisoner until I was old enough to find the scissors and cut it myself. "Okay," she said, "it's agreed upon, love pie," and when she started pushing the stroller again, the wheels went straighter and we moved faster, though on a rutted dirt road that even the county wouldn't claim, there was no such thing as speed.

Months before I was born, my mother had mail-ordered that stroller and x'ed off the days on Hinkley's Feed and Grain calendar until it arrived. "You won't be able to use it out here," my father had told her, but my mother was determined to do things right, to push me in a stroller like any other baby, despite the fact that the nearest sidewalk or park was a rough forty miles away. She used to tell people that we lived an hour and a half from nowhere, on a rocky ranch headed for no good, and she was just about right. In the southwest corner of Utah, amidst backcountry that was hallucinogenic in its loneliness and landscape, my father's family had slowly carved out a ranch.

The stroller proved difficult but not unmanageable out there, though my mother, that morning, had only one hand to use. When the wheels stopped in the ruts or hit loose dirt, she placed her hip against the handle, pushed hard with all of her one hundred and fifteen pounds, and got us moving again.

Who can really know the exact moment when something begins, but my mother's opinion is that the real trouble with my father had started months before when Milo de Rossi's car drove up, dust flying, the horn honking, two girls in the back seat tangled up with de Rossi in a way that was still illegal in this state. He introduced the girls as actresses.

Later, my mother looked at my father and scowled and, because her hands were full of wet laundry, blew a piece of hair tiredly away from her forehead. "Warren," she said, "let me ask you this. How many movies do you think those girls have been in?"

He stuck his hand in his back pocket, as if to get more room for thinking, and before he could answer, she continued. "Looks like they got the auditioning down."

Milo de Rossi had been looking for a place to film his next movie and he'd heard about our ranch and the land it sat on: red cliffs, deep canyons and the stark Bull Mountains in the distance. He found our land to be a cheap and ready-made set, just as other producers had discovered it and made it fit their needs. With a few props and the right camera angles, our ranch had been alternately transformed during the early 1950s into the Sahara, the moon, the Apache nation, and a hidden Mexican outpost filled with copper-faced desperados. In one of the lowest budget films ever, my father watched cavemen battle dinosaurs in the mock prehistoric valley just below our house, and everything in those ten days of filming would have been perfect, had my father not got into a shoving match with a caveman who, during a break, flirtingly lifted the edge of my mother's skirt with his spear and then grunted.

Milo de Rossi was not the first director to visit us, to shake my father's hand, and make a deal, but he was the first to tempt him. "And by the way," he had said to him casually, "we might be able to use you in a few scenes that haven't been fully written yet." De Rossi backed up, squared his hands out in front of his face to make a fleshy lens through which to look my father over. "Turn to the left, Warren, and lift your chin a little." My father complied, looking straight into the sun, squinting in a way that would later become Clint Eastwood's searing trademark.

They say that acting is a bug that bites, and if that's true, then my mother could tell you how that bite makes a person sick. My father didn't run a fever after de Rossi left, but he was as hot and irrational as a child with the flu.

"Honey," my mother tried to tell him, "the movies are a long shot. And you can't trust those people."

But my father had taken up staring at the horizon. He rode his horse and irrigated and cut hay and worked hard like he always did, though de Rossi had planted a tantalizing idea out in front of him. And around that time my mother noticed how often he was combing his hair. Any reflective surface would do: a fender, a piece of glass, the still surface of water. By then de Rossi and his crew were due back in three weeks.

We didn't wait for bad news to collapse around us. When my father had turned ice cold that morning and said that his mind was made up, that he'd take whatever de Rossi would give him and that he'd work his way up from there, my mother set her shoulders, let him have one last look at us, and headed out.

The sun was warm and she had stopped to give me

a bottle of water. "Hey sweet meat, we're doing fine," she said, kissed both my arms, tickled the warm wet spot under my chin, and pushed the stroller on. The breeze quickened and the cedars waved. A sugar-fine pelting of dust blew over my mother's ankles and between the stroller wheels, and from some indeterminate distance we heard a cow bellowing, low and sorrowful, then echoing back to itself off the high sandstone cliffs.

Some said the sky turned liquid; others, that it flexed and burned like at the beginning of time, but what we had seen from our ranch many times before were sudden long flashes as if a huge brilliant light had been turned on and then off in the distance. Ninety-eight miles away as the birds fly was the Nevada Test Site and in the middle of that was Yucca Flat, ground zero. From hillsides on our property, we had watched the explosions of test bombs Ruth, Dixie, Ray, Badger, and Simon. Sometimes we packed fruit or a small picnic to take along, we threw an old blanket on the ground, stretched out and waited, but we had grown bored with those events, stopped watching and accepted the bulletins which said everything was safe.

That morning, predawn, 1953, as part of the series of bombs codenamed Upshot-Knothole, Harry had been detonated, a shot that was named to sound as if you were talking about a friendly next-door neighbor. It hung from a 300-foot steel tower out there on Yucca Flat. At the end of the countdown, soldiers positioned three miles away as first-hand observers heard a loud click and then felt the raving heat of a new sun. They had been ordered down on one knee, left arms tight over their closed eyes, heads tucked. In those first two seconds of Harry, some of them saw the bones in their own arms—everywhere a huge luminous x-ray spreading outward. The ground shook and then the shock wave hit, knocking some of the men back, a wave that they eerily felt pass right through their bodies, front to back. And then the sound.

Some soldiers put their hands over their ears, though they had been instructed to keep their eyes covered. Others held their heads against the intense pressure of the blast. They felt a sudden heat in places like their kneecaps and the backs of their hands, and a slow—almost pleasant—tingling in their crotches that shortly, however, turned to painful needling. A private first class jumped up, hollering, holding himself between his legs, but a buddy pulled him back down where he crouched and covered his head and moaned.

Little by little the roaring diminished and the soldiers' heads came up. They uncovered their ears and were ordered to stand. By that time darkness was ebbing and against the mauve sky they saw a swirling golden fireball, alive, kinetic. The gaseous ring around it shimmered red, green, and blue and even the most nervous and frightened soldiers saw it as beautiful, mesmerizing. They watched as the fireball was lifted higher and higher in a mass of roiling gray-black clouds, which didn't mush-room as they usually did, but spread and then drifted. A sergeant yelled for the men to doubletime it into nearby assault vehicles, and when loaded, they headed for ground zero. They drove past a line of mannequins that had been planted upright on metal poles. The man-nequins had been suited up in utility jackets and helmets, and then placed in formation like a scraggly half-wit battalion. The helmets were blown off, the jackets burn-ing, and the mannequin faces melted into flesh-colored pools onto the desert floor. The vehicles slowed. Some of the soldiers laughed as they went by, but most were quiet.

Not far from there they passed a small reconnais-sance team already at work herding pigs out of an experi-mental trench. These were important pigs. They wore specially tailored uniforms that were made from a new synthetic fabric that the Army was testing, supposedly durable and lightweight, a promise for all future soldiers. The scientists were disappointed when they failed to train the pigs to stand on hind legs—more closely simu-lating humans—but the moment that Harry went off, the pigs were suddenly upright, standing, squealing, urinat-ing, front hooves pawing the air. Dogs, monkeys and burros were also somewhere out there being monitored in dry underground bunkers.

Closing in on ground zero—less than half a mile—the sparse landscape turned empty. Trucks and equipment that had been left there were gone, everything flash-burned into the minute particles that fell, ash-like, here and there as a strange rain. Five hundred yards out the assault vehicles stopped, the rear ramps lowered, the soldiers disembarked, and began to move in formation up the incline where the detonation tower, now vaporized, had stood. The ground everywhere was winter white, but hot. Above them, the desert dawn had been erased by heavy black clouds, smoke, floating debris.

Two hundred yards from center they stopped, and having fulfilled their orders and not knowing now exactly what to do, the sergeant stepped out front, smartly saluted ground zero, turned, and ordered the men to head back. With each heavy booted step, the snowy dust and ash floated up so that from a distance the men looked as if they were moving, knee-deep, through clouds.

Elly and Lewis Barlow, our neighbors, were card players—experts at Hearts and No Knock Rummy; tender for a game that they had taught my parents called Michigan. Winter nights the four of them would be hunched over a kitchen table, moaning about what they'd been dealt. My mother never held her cards in close enough and oftentimes my father got a peek at the Queen of Spades or at a run or he'd push her hand toward her chest and give her a warning. "Lorraine, you're showing us everything."

"Well, not everything," she'd say, putting her cards

down and starting to unbutton her blouse. Lewis smacked his cards face down and clapped. Elly squealed and took the time to roll a cigarette—Prince Albert in a can. My father got up from the table, stood behind my mother and wrapped his arms around her, as if that was the only way she could be stopped. "Okay, okay," he said, "I'm sorry."

Actually, my parents were wrapped around each other like that almost half the time—embracing, clutching, hugging, pawing. With other men, my mother said she would have felt mauled, but with my father, she felt her heart race, she felt her shoes suddenly wanting to be thrown off. They had sex like animals and she was not ashamed to say so: on a living room chair, in the root cellar, in the orchard during spring when the ribbon grass was still soft enough to make a bed. Nearby, I dozed or chewed my fist and waited.

My mother knew that leaving wouldn't be easy, and maybe that's another reason we headed for the Barlows that morning: comfort and an understanding shoulder. Elly and Lewis had lived a fairly bumpy life themselves— fast times and booze in Vegas casinos—and they looked on other people's trouble with gentle eyes.

My mother gauged that we had gone over two miles and were more than halfway there. We had passed the S-curve in the road a while back and she thought we must be close to Carpenter Wash, but time and long brown vistas mingled and distorted both. She prodded the stroller to the side of the road, found a flat rock and we sat facing each other.

"Huh, movies," she said. "What baloney. What trash."

Months before at a nearby filming site where my father was caring for the horses used in breakneck cavalry scenes, my mother had met a brawny blonde named Jeff Cantrell, an in-demand lead for B Movies, and she was thoroughly unimpressed. Brusque and egotistical, he spent too much time dabbing perspiration from his face and yelling for someone to bring him iced tea, and when she learned that his real name was Ira Kaufmann, she was even more disgusted. "What, is he ashamed to use his real name?" she wanted to know. All the hubbub and shouting around the set didn't seem to foster any character in those people as far as she was concerned. Everyone was either whining or cussing or laughing with the fake high-pitched laughter that she identified as Hollywood.

Milo de Rossi hadn't shown her anything different. My father had escorted him around our ranch for several days, pointing out box canyons and high rocky fortresses, and by the second day de Rossi was convinced that this was the place for his movie, *Apache Sunset*. He already had Audie Murphy lined up, he said. He hoped for Anthony Quinn or Lee Marvin as the sad-eyed Apache leader who would glimpse the future and see the pain for which his people were bound. De Rossi was still new enough in the business to be regarded with hope, but his lack of financial foresight and his thudding story lines would finally catch up with him, and in the years ahead he was destined for junk.

Smoking fat Havana Cristo's, he took pleasure in confiding to everyone at dinner each night: William Holden had a drinking problem; sometimes had to be thrown in a shower before he could complete his scenes.

My mother shook her head as she served the venison or roast she had carefully prepared. Everyone ate as if they'd been deprived for months.

"Kirk Douglas?" he asked. "Know him? Gotta hire a full-time tutor to teach him his lines. Sorta like training a dog, I guess. A little thin between the old ears. Of course, this is only what I hear. I'm just passing it along."

My mother couldn't stand de Rossi's feral gaze when anything female moved past him. "Call me Milo, my dear," he had told her as she bent over the oven pulling out hot rolls.

"If I had the chance, I'd call him a lot worse than that," she told me as we sat at the side of the road. Her shoulder-length dark hair blew forward around her face, and with one hand she quickly gathered it up and held it at the back of her neck. With the other, she moved the stroller back and forth, gently rocking me in the sunshine. I babbled my heart out to her, kicked my feet, and squirmed in the cotton netting of the seat and these things she understood as my wanting to get back on the road. She picked up the suitcase, turned the stroller around and shoved us forward.

By then, in the far-off distance ahead, the sky was changing and at first my mother wasn't concerned—a hundred changes rolled by each day in that enormous unpredictable sky—but as the disturbance came closer, she pushed more firmly against the stroller. From the first good look, she could see that it was not the deep pouting gray of a thunderhead. It was another one of those churning purple-black clouds from the test site, but it was larger this time and lower. In it, she saw sparks of light, glimmerings, electricity, she didn't know what.

"Nothing to worry about," she told me, though I wasn't worried. I was happy, totally entertained. The scenery slipped by, right and left, like wavy blue-and-brown streamers. I pointed randomly and screeched.

"Tree," she said. "Rock." "Fence." "Horse." "Mountain." She reeled off a vocabulary that I was at least a good six months away from, but she encouraged me to try anyway. She loved the sound of me, unlike Miss Lurl, my third grade teacher who years later put tape over my mouth. "Miss Yakety Yak" she called me, and my schoolmates picked it up, chanted it at recess, whispered it down the rows at the spelling bee.

My mother and I passed Carpenter Wash and then the wind grew stronger and came in bursts. My mother's skirt clung to the front of her legs and flared out in back, waving behind her. She stopped, dug through the suit-case, took out a lacy white bonnet and put it on me, drawing it down low over my forehead, tying the straps firmly beneath my soft clefted chins, which she couldn't resist pinching. My mother loved all of me, but it was my head that she had high hopes for and therefore pro-tected—a bonnet, a scarf, a ratty straw hat used for gardening. Sometimes, in the heat, she put a wet cloth on my head, water dripping down my neck and shoul-ders, my face scrunching up into a good cry, but she hushed me without any sympathy. She wanted me to be able to think, to reason, which is where the trouble lay for her.

My mother didn't have to reason that morning, how-ever. A mother simply tastes trouble; she feels it in the small of her back or in her blood or somewhere along her jangly nerves. Even ten miles off and blowing toward her, trouble was about as discreet as an ocean liner full of singing drunks. My mother said she suddenly smelled something carried on the wind: lye and dust and burnt liver or kidney beans, an awful combination that made her gasp. She hadn't eaten much that morning, and her stomach turned once and then she got ahold of herself. She dropped the suitcase right there in the road as if it was something that had become crude and pointless, and with both hands on the stroller, she started running, barreling into the wind, pushing us madly up a small ridge from where, she hoped, we might be able to see the Barlows' windmill. The stroller wheels kept hitting rocks and ruts, but she powered through, sending the stroller sideways and the front end off the ground. I slid down in the seat, crumpled formless as a pillow, laughed and squealed and did my best to kick away my shoes.

On the broad Lincoln County range that runs from Nevada head-on into western Utah, sheep were grazing. The bells they wore jingled like a soft stuttering music out in no-man's land. These were Western sheep, medium-sized and perseverant, muzzles down in sagebrush and galleta grass. Though spread out and foraging, they still moved as a loose, everpresent herd.

The cloud blew over about nine that morning. The wind came with it, blowing to the east and then suddenly shifting north, stirring up dust devils, rolling tumbleweeds across the desert into the midst of the feeding sheep. They scattered with the noise and sudden movement. As the sky overhead turned dark, sheep dashed for cover that wasn't there. The bells on their necks clattered wildly, bringing more confusion and panic. A fine dusty mist began to fall from the cloud, and like rain, covered and penetrated: the dense layered wool of the sheep, the heavy leafed sage. The sheep veered right and left, stumbled and doubled back on themselves, and even after the cloud had passed, the bleating continued. They hopped and skittered at a falling rock, at a shadow, at a waving branch. Finally they lowered their heads again, though the ground and plants were now covered with a film of ash which lent a strange new taste to sagebrush. Slowly they grazed their way into the next valley.

Not far away in Elgin, Nevada, three children came out of a trailer house and played in what they imagined to be snow. They spread their arms, ran in circles, and turned their faces up into the gray-white storm. The oldest one—the only one who could write—used her finger to trace her name through the snow collecting on the hood of a junked car in the driveway. She licked her finger to clean it and then cartwheeled while the two younger ones, in wet drooping diapers, made themselves dizzy spinning.

From there the cloud moved due east—Nevada into Utah, though there was no marked change from one place to the other. It was all just dry unrelenting terrain. Here and there, almost like accidents, a tarpapered house sprang up and next to it the rotted posts of an abandoned corral, and in those lonely places, a Basque shepherd or a used car salesman holding a geiger counter looked up, wondered to himself, and shrugged.

A young husband, hauling furniture in his truck from Veyo to Santa Clara, was surprised by how the cloud seemed to engulf him and even to move with him down Highway 18. He'd driven in weather before, sometimes been able to outrun the big spring and summer cloudbursts if he caught them far enough on the horizon in time. Ten miles out of Veyo, though, this cloud had caught him, surrounding the truck in whirling sand.

Particles hit the windshield and seeped through every crevice of the old Ford until even his clothes were covered with a fine light soot.

When he finally turned off the side road and moved onto Highway 91, which led into Santa Clara and then on into Las Vegas, he was surprised to find a roadblock set up at a Texaco station. He shifted down, idled forward, then stopped his truck and got out. Hours later, before the young man was allowed to go, the deputies burned his clothes, patted his shoulder to reassure him, and let him borrow a Texaco uniform to wear home. Even with her own furniture in the back of the truck, his wife didn't know him when he drove up to their house and stepped out of the cab.

My mother's lungs burned from running. Her arms and shoulders felt disconnected and one of her ankles was swelling, and by then she realized the stroller wasn't worth the trouble. She picked me up out of it, wrapped me in her arms and she wished, for once, that there was more of her to cradle and cover me. She had run herself out, so she trotted on from there, off balance and heavy footed, alternately watching the sky and the road and me.

Coming in fast from the southwest, the cloud grew larger, its edges spreading like thin fingers. In the mid-morning sky, it appeared to be a piece of boiling twilight that had broken away from somewhere else. Instinctively my mother moved over to the far side of the road, putting a little more distance between it and us.

I worked my arm away from my mother's chest and touched her chin and talked to her in code—coos and broken syllables and among them she was almost positive that she heard the name John. Had the moment been different, she would have stopped, sat me in her lap, and we would have had a heart-to-heart, but as it was, we kept going.

My mother had shaken John Wayne's hand and that was about all. He was making arrangements for his upcoming movie, *The Conqueror*, in which he would play Genghis Khan and tempt Susan Hayward with his made-up almond eyes. It would be filmed not far from our ranch and he wanted to look things over, make some plans for his sons who would accompany him. Someone had given him a cup of coffee. My mother remembered Wayne stirring in two teaspoons of sugar and drinking the coffee so slowly that it had to be ice cold when he got to the bottom. He nodded his head shyly when they were introduced, stood up out of his chair and extended his hand and she could see that he was a big, sensitive meatblock of a man.

Sometimes in panic and in trying to protect our life, my mother forgot things about the movies: the sweet temperate nature of John Wayne, the way Milo de Rossi had written my father a large check for his and my mother's hospitality and it was that very check that gave us Christmas that year. My mother unwrapped her dream of a sewing machine and cried on and off all day.

A mother's intuition is seldom wrong and my mother's was always right about her babies. If she was mostly right about Milo de Rossi, she was absolutely right about that cloud. We had to find shelter.

She had taken only two steps off the road—toward a feeble overhang in the rocks—when she heard the long frantic blasts of a horn. My father, like a man driven by deep stinging forces that we couldn't understand, had ingeniously spliced the ignition on the old Dodge flatbed and gunned his way to find us. His puzzlement and fear had grown by leaps as he found first the suitcase in the road and then the abandoned stroller.

At the sound of the horn my mother turned and scanned the road behind until finally she could see the grill and the familiar green hood and the brown trail of road dust. She put her arm in the air and waved.

When finally he was next to us, my father opened his door, the engine still running, and came around and opened the other door for us. They didn't say a word, didn't give each other the cool slender glance of people still carrying grudges. With me held closer than ever to her chest, my mother skip-hopped onto the running board and then up onto the seat, looked straight ahead and waited for my father to slam the door.

He, of course, thought she was coming back for him. He couldn't stand two hours without her and he thought she felt the same, and in a while, she did. But at the moment when she had jumped into the truck, she was all mother, all pounding heart, and she didn't for one second analyze our escape.

We drove back to the house while behind us, in the valley to the west, in the very spot where *The Conqueror* would be filmed the next year, the cloud unloaded sheer white dust and here and there glassy particles that would end up driving the camera men wild, sudden glints and glarings appearing in the uncut footage. Sitting in the truck that day, we didn't know it, but my father would be there at that filming, too, maybe not a star but at least an extra. For weeks, dressed in blousy Mongol pants and wearing snow boots, he was destined to ride a skiddish buckskin a hundred times across the same stretch of red sand until someone finally yelled that they had a take.

My father, glad to have his wife and daughter back that day, drove carefully and watched in his rearview mirror; my mother kept turning around. They didn't know exactly what they were seeing back there, but they were spooked, and in no time she had slid across the seat and partnered back up with him. The cloud hung low for a while and didn't seem to move. Beneath it, wind and dust and fallout created a turbulent hothouse that we could see and would hear about on the radio the next day.

Maybe to calm herself, my mother started—right there in the truck—by kissing my father's cheek, even though it was a little too smooth for her taste, a little too much like a young James Stewart's. Then things fell into place: a kiss, a hug, and my mother's skirt coming up over her legs.

As my father was trying to drive with one hand, trying to sneak quick views of the road ahead, I told him, in the only way that I could—with grunts and aaahs and jibberish—that I loved him, whatever he was going to be.

In the months and years that followed after we safely arrived home, Telsa was exploded, Priscilla, Diablo, and Hood. There were others we didn't learn the names of. They drifted overhead, engraving a darkness in the sky, but in time they only appeared to pass and move into the shimmering distance.

# three

# NEVADA BORDER TOWNS

*Marcelyn Ritchie*

Will and I have never done a truly bold thing. We came here to this bar in Baker, Nevada, because something kept us from driving further. It is a friendly, meatloaf-on-Monday kind of place. Beer is only a buck, unless you are gambling, then it's free. Will says, "Gamble, make a maneuver to gain an advantage." Will likes to talk like that. His left hand reaches for me as his right drops in quarters, then pushes "deal." Will's hands are not what drew me to him. His fingers are thick and there is a pink scab forming near his left index finger knuckle. I follow past his hands, past his baby smooth elbow to that place between his shoulder and his neck, that place my head is drawn to. Today, maneuvering to gain advantage means moving from my blackjack machine to the one next to him. "Endure to completion," is what my grandmother Rose would say, "be his stay, a steadying thing."

Being Rose's first granddaughter means I get that kind of advice. It also means I count cards and I am stubborn. Staying, right now, requires more than just anteing up.

Rose thinks she is sixteen. My mother says to me, "Follow Rose's eyes in the pictures before she was married." What Rose eyes is my short hair cut and my leather skirt. Once when I walked into her house wearing that skirt she asked to borrow it. She said, "Treasure," that's Rose's nickname for me, "slip it off, let me try it on." Rose maneuvers me away from my mother so she can whisper rules to me: "Never leave it to chance to fill your dance program," and "Notice who looked away first." My mother asks: "What does Rose tell you?"

My mother and Rose share tips about wearing bright lipstick and walking fast. "So people will notice," my mother says. Stares mean more to these women than getting any rewards in heaven. They both burned their journals and cards from old lovers. I see my mother and Rose squatting on spiked heels in front of a brick fireplace. Burning the evidence. But facts remain, those glossy smiles.

Will and I gamble at home, the home that Rose deeded me promising the gabled roof and scalloped window dormers would shield me. Will comes home early from the four-star restaurant where he is the head chef and maneuvers me to the front porch. He unties his apron and balls it under my head, the smell of pesto and marinara sticky in my hair. He sucks through my shirt then pulls it off, straining the seams and stretching elastic. He hurries at first and then he lingers. He takes my face in his hands, ripe fruit, his fingers covering my eyes and kisses me. He licks at my welling tears. Nothing distracts Will. On our porch just before dusk, me in only my pink bra, Will hard against me, not even the possibility of 7 x 35 binoculars slow him. He knows some neighbor guy could be focusing on the space that doesn't exist between us. A round circle bleeding to two when we move, twisting, my leg caught under his as his neck bends around mine.

Will's game of choice is Craps. You win with money on the Come line. We've made all the jokes. But there are only formica-top tables in Baker, none with felt and fake wood. So Will plays my game. Blackjack. And he splits on nines and tens, making me crazy.

Rose whispers words like vows: gown, ribbon, velvet. These words with red in front of them flush her liver-splotched cheeks. And Rose cries. Mention Jews or the spot she lost as Wasatch High valedictorian and she'll search up her sleeve or under her fabric-covered belt for her handkerchief.

Rose and my mother and I play Rook on Saturday afternoons, never Hearts. Face cards, the King and Queen of Hell, are not allowed. "That reminds me," Rose will say, and my mother will laugh. Rose is famous to those who know her for outbidding her hand. Men and cards, she always thought they'd win her more, more than a mediocre Widow.

"We need a game plan," Will says.

"The women of my family need to be pretty," I say.

"Audrey, just take my hand," he says.

We're standing outside that bar in Baker, Nevada, on the loneliest road in the country. It is not a hazardous gambling town. There is no Red Garter casino and no golf course. And you can't squander much without those felt-covered tables. But more is on the line. Will wants a word from me, a nod. I bow my head and tuck both fists under my chin. He knows to quick-as-a-dealer's-shuffle pull me against his chest.

Rose wants me to do something other than hold my cards. She passes along advice by pointing out magazine articles. "Treasure, cut them out," she says as she kinder-garten-hands me scissors: "Grown Ups Who Were Spoiled Growing Up," "Dancing: The Best Exercise in High Heels," and "Beware Men Bearing Roses."

What Rose is trying to tell me isn't quite clear. I do know this hand should be a hold and I know this thing between Will and me isn't fully dealt. I don't know much more except Will doesn't look me in the eye and I don't arch against him from behind as he places only his suitcase in the trunk. There are things you just don't do on the day the man leaving you against your will, leaves.

Rose worries I inherited her weak heart. She worries I give it away in every Nevada border town. Rose wants me to have memories, like pressed roses, that I can share with my children and grandchildren. "They are waiting to be born," she says, "you must think of them."

Staying in Baker without Will isn't a hand to risk on a house bust. But I've stayed with less. "Treasure, a good Widow can change a hand." Standing in the parking lot of that small bar in Baker I cross my eyes blurring the circle a hawk is traveling waiting to catch a thermal. Minutes pass. The green of Wheeler Peak melts into the hot, low desert. Will pauses at the intersection waiting for all the lonely traffic already heading east. He U-turns sharp and pulls up beside me. He gets out of the car and walks towards me but he leaves the car running. It idles fast, the hawk circles slowly above us. My arms are two wings anchored by my hands snug in my back pockets. "Watch for those arcs, the ones with seven prismatic colors," Will says. He releases my right arm and it springs out, cutting the air. Will isn't giving me practical advice. He is talking about atmospheric patterns and about how I always find luck just when. Will shimmies apart my feet with his scuffed boot. My center of gravity shifts. Will leaves.

Rose's grandmother, Renee, was Basque and she liked being alone. Renee lost her teenage husband weeks after he got her pregnant. Renee then said yes to a polygamist. He got her pregnant too. Many times. She went crazy, which is not what her granddaughter Rose would say. Rose would say, "Ma had a tendency concerning geography."

It's a long walk to Salt Lake and I shouldn't have let myself get staked out here alone. You could say it happened because of last night. I knew shutting the motel door softly behind me at midnight and not opening it again till dawn was only one way, but a sure one of putting real space between now and the someday of buying a ranch in central Nevada with Will.

The fact is, Renee would wander in the Utah hills in the winter. She usually left on horse, one named Adversity or maybe Zion, and came back on foot.

Here, the sun is setting red over Wheeler Peak. Somewhere in central Utah Will is driving four miles over the speed limit listening to some woman describe her missing daughter on talk radio. Me, I'm low on aces wandering in the desert. Fact: I'm sitting on a bar stool eating a meatloaf sandwich and considering my own tendencies, geography certainly being one of them. The jukebox plays a lot of George Jones and songs about lost clothing, buttons, and boots missing without a trace. At each entrance of a steel guitar I cover my mouth and suck in one hard breath.

When Will gets home he'll pack some things into his canvas laundry bag—the one he had in college. The one that says, "Shit, it's only dirt" on the outside. He'll think of me in the chipped paint motel in Baker but he won't come back. He won't wire money. Will understands the ways I am most like Rose. He knows that for us, having our way means we first must think of it.

Will has the scars from pushing too hard. He knows I'll make a deal, steal a horse, get home somehow. He worries but he won't preempt luck. He'll wait. He knows that when I bend forward, my hair covering my right eye, I can tip a hand.

Rose wanders too. She married a man she didn't quite love because his eyes followed her as she walked. Renee told Rose, "Love is only a decision to stop moving." Rose walked a lot. She'd start heading south and follow any street till it ended. Then she'd sit for a while until my grandfather pulled up, stopping short. We got calls. He was late a few times.

Too often I sluff the card I need. Hitchhiking is not what Rose would suggest. She'd say, "Don't count on Roses in December." I take Greyhound and I make it home.

Rose was wild. My mother says Rose must have been susceptible to charm. Rose was caught kissing a Park City boy at the Saltair dance pavilion when the lights came on. Park City boys were better dancers after all. She won dance contests all over the state: 5-pound boxes of Blue-bird chocolates and first prize when she danced at Geneva pavilion on the Utah Lake shore. She has ribbons. Rose says, "Secrets are the things worth growing O-L-D for." Sharing them is what my mother and Rose did, in the dark after I'd gone to sleep, littering my dreams.

My mother led me to Rose. "She has stories to tell," my mother said. My mother looks like Rose, even though she is only her daughter-in-law. Their eyebrows curve, penciled in cathedral arches. Rose and my mother compare pictures of themselves in their fast twenties. "You must never," Rose says when I walk into the room. "No, never," my mother says. "What?" I ask. They sit on Rose's couch and lean over the coffee table. In the pictures they both had painted lips and tight curls on their foreheads.

At home I knock, then use my key. Will is balled up on the floor with my pink bra wrapped around his closed fist. "You need some sun," I say.

"Some black olive pesto," he says.

"I can't deal with this."

"Hold the hand you came with," Rose would say.

The this I refer to is the us before it was split like two aces in a little town on the loneliest road in the country. But I'm not mad and we're not mean. We've just reached the point where being kind has hurt us more than anything else. I kneel by Will and open his hands. He twirls my ring. "Stay," Will says as he lifts that wayward strand of hair out of my face and tucks it behind my ear. The afternoon sun through the aluminum-framed window is warm on my back. I shake my head.

"There was a diamond," he says.

"Notice when I stop moving," I say. I leave.

I stand in my mother's bathroom, spinning. Grief, to my mother, is one more excuse to apply make-up. "Just imagine Rose," my mother says. I peer into the mirror.

My mother motions like a game-show hostess, pointing at all the drawers that hold what could make me so much closer to beautiful. She points to the vanishing cream, her red lipstick, her eyelash curler. My mother tells her friends, "That Audrey, she fixes up real nice and she can change her own oil." My mother has secrets too. She purses her lips when anyone mentions apple orchards or cable cars. An engraved white Bible sits on her bed stand—her last gift from her first love. She tells me I am lucky to be a tall woman from a line of thin ones. She says, "Audrey, play your high card."

How we ended up in this car without questions, only statements, is simple. "We'll drive," Will had said.

"I'm not staying alone," I said.

"Stay on a soft 17," he said.

Will tosses chicken bones into the back seat. We pass the exit to the airport and where we are going is the only place left to go on this road with a half tank of gas. Rose would say that I'm playing a Nellow Rook hand with no ones.

I hold my hand in front of Will's face. My fingers are long. Will says they are the longest he's ever seen. Will says, "Point to the glacier scar line." I trace a line in the fog on Will's window. With his hand that is not on the wheel, he takes my finger. He pulls until the knuckle pops. Lightning starts out on the flats. I lean against the cold glass and count. Will makes sizzling sounds.

We pull into the Red Garter. Will collects quarters from under the mat and the glove box. I brought bills. I've got a fair stack to lose. "Don't let me throw away the gas money," Will says.

"Don't let me bet my rings," I say.

"Play conservative with 13s," Will says.

Around the metal legs of the stool my feet are cold. Will stands behind me leaning against my sloped spine. His hands rub my shoulders. He adds my cards and his hands stiffen. "Beware gambling with your own weak heart," Rose would say. My bangs are in my eyes, leaving only a slat of light. I push back against Will's large palms. "Stay," he says. Hitting and staying, doubling and splitting, that's all there is in twenty-one. My back is cold. His weight is no longer balancing mine.

The woman sitting next to me is losing even bigger than I am. Her bets are large and she hesitates more than a kid on the high dive. She's taking hits with the dealer showing a four. She's third base and she's messing up the way the cards land.

"My boyfriend can't stand to watch me lose," she says.

"Where is he?" I say.

"Over by yours," she says.

"Mine," I say.

The dealer spreads his fingers outside the circle where my green $25 chips lay. I haven't bet the porch yet.

It's light outside. Will has won bills and thrown away change. I just stopped. Will noticed.

"I feel for those who call this town home," I say.

"We're not driving back," Will says.

"Ever," I say.

Will won enough to pay the $29.95 week-day room rate. If he wanted me to chip in he never asked. We drive to the last motel on the east side of town. If there was ever cause to investigate, it might appear we started to leave town then changed our minds. Not exactly the order things took.

Will is quiet in the bathroom. No running water, not even a cough. Now isn't the time to bluff. Rose lost the diamond from her wedding ring after she tried to tell my grandfather he was just too simple to love. She sat on the floor, her nightgown pulled over her knees. The spiky edge of her ring caught. They spent the rest of the night searching.

I wake up as the sun is setting. Against me Will's body is warm. "Treasure, unless you double-Nellow, your partner doesn't get to play." Rose is famous for Nellowing alone. Will's back is to me but his feet are wrapped around mine. As I move he grips my feet with his. He is my stay. My grandfather bought Rose a new diamond with money saved from their laundromat. Not wanting it didn't matter. They stayed together for another forty years.

# four

# SOME BODY PARTS REMEMBER A WAR

*Nicole Stansbury*

A woman with teeth, with teeth, with hair. A stage singer and when she sang her legs rolled like water like she had no kneecaps plus she wore a shiny blue man's silk suit and underneath it, without kneecaps, those crazy hoppin' rollin' legs drove you wild with happiness. And all around you were girls who loved her just the same as you; who threw roses onstage and blew kisses and held their chests like their hearts would bust right out. Like they were at a Beatles concert maybe. But the woman just sang and sang and sang. She sang: When it's sugar cane time, around about noon, I'll be walkin' with my Sugar, 'neath that old sugar moon. And how when she sang she'd be walkin' with her Sugar, her lips slid off her teeth, she smiled like she was thinking of somebody, and you and everybody in the audience could see it. Try to imagine them, the stage singer with dark hair glistening and high and spiky on her head and some woman, blonde, wearing a bright plastic red lei. Walking. Holding hands. Kissing. Her knees rolled! She galloped across the stage, still singing, and then slid right onto her side like someone coming into home! She was still singing lying there flat on her back and who knows what might've occurred to her looking up into those hot humongous white lights. Well and the crowd went wild. And the singer sat up, combed her hair flat with her fingers, hit a long low note a most amazing long low note; sat propped on her side and saw a child sleeping in the audience. So the singer sat up and walked to the edge of the stage and said to the dad of the little girl: did we lose her? And the little girl who'd fallen asleep with arms and hair hanging back now looked like a corpse against her dad's chest, even amongst the screaming loving fans who threw so many piles of roses, swaddled in cellophane, enormous and crackling. The singer had to step around them the way you step around doo dahs on a miniature golf course.

What you do is go to Lake Tahoe where she has her next concert and you're wearing red tights, the reddest tights of all, with pale green cowboy boots which don't match but who cares since this, this giving over and giving in to her, is surely the purest joy you've ever known. Walkin' in those boots makes your hips swing! Find the casino she's staying in. Write to your friends, say: I'd never heard such a thing! as the way the notes came out of her mouth. As the way her mouth moved around in her face like she was eating canaries and angels all at the same time. Oh, my. Your brother tells you on the phone she is terrible-looking, why doesn't she at least wear some earrings. Think of all the self-mutilations you've seen, in magazines and real life: your own earlobes, a woman in a biker magazine who'd pierced her genitals. The woman wore a silver hoop and a chain which was held by a hand at the edge of the photograph. She was smiling, looking proud.

Get off the phone and wait in the lobby, hoping to get a glimpse. The bellhop has fallen in love with you he has no idea. He admires your tights. He admires your red nails. He knows things about the singer, like that she's on the sixteenth floor and a very friendly person, a very genuine person he says, though he has never seen her sing and howl and slide, never seen the roll and sweep of this same singer's legs. He has never noticed maybe such straight white teeth and cheekbones which give her appearance an Aleutian cast, that's what you think, or even sort of a fetal cast. What you mean is her features are smooth and low-lying, like she wasn't quite through growing into her face before she got born. Try to explain this to the bellhop. He says, fetal? He touches one of your red fingernails, finally gets around to snapping the red nylon bunched over one kneecap after you stood up waiting on the couch in the lobby three hours, hoping for a glimpse.

On the street you have never felt so good so beautiful so madly in love and it makes you strut, the skies in Lake Tahoe are chlorine blue and a man sees you on the street. He's tromping towards you on the sidewalk, his boots sinking in snowdrifts and when you come even the man says, Do you work for the casino? he says, How much? The way you'd been smiling so big! The way you'd worn red tights just for the singer! Give him the bird. But later change into sedate pantyhose.

Send a letter up to the singer's room the morning of her second and last appearance in beautiful Lake Tahoe. Invite her to breakfast! At Denny's, tell the waitress: Two. The singer never shows up. Her legs roll and roll. Feel it in the place where you think your womb must be, though it's hard to know for sure.

Wait again in the lobby. Then here comes the singer: watch how she holds the heavy glass door for a blonde-haired woman carrying a huge plant. The singer, trying not to be noticed, makes a beeline for a red velvet sash beyond which is the auditorium. Your legs huff and puff getting to her though the trick is not to scare her off by seeming like a loony tunes fruitcake who could whip out a pistol any second. It happens to lots of celebrities and you're pretty sure she worries about it since why wouldn't she? But oh. But oh. Because now she's trapped behind the red sash, the auditorium door is locked so she's going to be looking at you any second. When she turns to say *What* in a tired voice, she's had it with adoring fans, remember lines from the *Waste Land,* remember: I could not speak, I was neither living nor dead and I knew nothing. Nothing. Remember, looking into the heart of light, the silence. Then the singer gets impatient, she says, What! This is when you realize she doesn't love you, can you believe it? Though since you first heard her songs it was like having a tiny invisible giraffe friend that hung out in your pocket who you were always trying to think up jokes for. See with shame that you're keeping her friend with the plant from even being able to escape to the elevators. Oh goodness the embarrassment and grief. Nothing can come out of your mouth. You can't even say I'm sorry.

One year later World War III happens. Rock-n-roll with the singer in secret love and privacy in your living room all the months in between. Catch an interview between the singer and Connie Chung where Connie wears earrings and tells the singer she dresses like a man. Catch the footage of missiles sailing through black skies into Iraq. On television no one will say how many people are dead instead they say our objectives have been satisfactorily achieved. She is a singer and has nothing in common with war; but somehow both things, the memory of her mouth and now the bodies flying, get you in the same way. Because anymore you can't tell where your heart is or your brain or even your own bowels. At some point, maybe that day in the casino or maybe these days watching Dan Rather's mouth, all the parts seem to have come loose and floated away from their moorings. At some point all the organs and bones remembered something and without asking, switched places. You could wake up tomorrow and find a kidney on your tongue. Find a kneecap scooting along your spine, trying for home. Catch the footage of more missiles making humongous white holes in a daytime sky. Catch the corpses. Think: lost, lost, we've lost her, all.

# five

# MOUTH TO MOUTH

*Shen Christenson*

I remember it often. It made national news: view after view of a woman, made-up, teeth and microphone shining, eyes on the story board; bloodstains. The mother rented a room on the fourteenth floor of the Tri-Arc Hotel where she knelt with her children all morning, whispering prayers. Then she led them out to the balcony and threw them down to the sidewalk. Kissed each one and said: fly, sweetheart. She jumped off after. She had no will. Left nothing, no note to be read. The baby was killed, of course, and all the others except the three-year-old girl, who had shattered legs and shards of bone in her brain, but the rest of her must have been cushioned by the pulp of her siblings. She is alive now, in a hospital back in Salt Lake, where she doesn't paint with a brush in her teeth, tell stories, sing; she masturbates in her wheelchair, rocks in her bed. I think about what those children might have thought in that moment between leaving the balcony and landing, what they saw spinning to the sidewalk. Did they scream or sigh?

The name of the hotel changed, but they didn't take off the skinny metal balconies. The picture is there, blood in my mouth, every time I look down from high places.

The father was never shown.

I have children of my own. Kate. Willow. Sammy. It's strangely hard sometimes, to remember them. They seem insubstantial. It's worse than catching a dream the next morning, where you don't know what's inside your head and what's not. My kids weren't on the T.V.

Pictures of them—to remember?

Kate grew like a sunflower, skinny and straight and hair poking up from her head in petals. Willow had squashy feet. I'd kiss them; I'd say, This little one cried all the way home. I try to think of Sammy, something good. And then I remember their father. It's like looking at an optical illusion, one of those black-and-white pictures that looks like a sweet-faced woman and a witch too—how once you see the face and the witch, you can't know how it was to see only the face.

To remember their father—I will not. When my kids spilled what their father had done, would do—when everything past fell out of my focus—I ran. Sam went in day care. The girls were in school. I went to work cleaning. It held us together. My mind had flown.

After a year I could read again. Magazines, anyway,

ladies and news ones. The words were things I could recognize. Although books with long plots, love lines— they still splat on what my girls told had happened, what's past, and seem senseless. The ad for the Clairol contest in *Family Circle* for mothers wanting to go back to school I understood. And thanks to Clairol we're in California and I don't clean anymore. You had to send in a Before Miss Clairol photo and an After. A lady I worked for, I'd pick up her dog's crap and get the stains out of her carpets and sheets; she'd work on my make-up. She'd decorate, then stand back and squint. Kate said about the After photograph: You look sort of pretty, in a fake way. Willow cried over the red hair and told me my crack showed—my cleavage, she meant, which Sam said looked like my butt was in the wrong place. But I looked a lot better than the Before and I won. They flew me from Price, Utah, to New York to get the scholarship, and they made me over again and took a new picture. It came out on a page called *et cetera*, black-and-white, small, with the winning women all so competently lovely, I wasn't sure which After was me.

So I moved the four of us to Berkeley; not too close to Disneyland, and the university didn't request self-evaluations, they cared what you could score. I'm taking Evolution and the Fossil Record, Conversational French, Problems in Population Development, Meteorology, Human Sexuality and Its Pursuit. Things like that make a lot of sense to me; I used to believe in religion.

Laundry day. A sheet pinned between my chin and chest.

"Mommy," Willow asks me, "are you having more babies?"

"You have to have a dad, stupid," Kate says, not looking up from the book open across her knees.

"Well, Mom could get a dad. Couldn't you?"

"No," Kate says. "Shut-up."

"Mommy could marry Hobb. Couldn't you?" Willow asks me.

"His head is shaped like a lightbulb," Kate says.

"Hobb says there is heaven," Willow tells her.

"You have no taste," Kate says. "Mom's not getting married. We're normal."

I believe that. At least I do when I go up University Boulevard, past Shattuck. There's always students doing stuff like taking off their clothes to celebrate the sun and waving poster boards, trying to change things; Sammy and Willow use the old poster board signs for forts. There is a science professor who only has half a face. I see him everywhere. The other half got burned up in a fusion experiment. There are lots of dogs, Hare Krishnas, and too many trees.

Most of the time I think moving here was a clean break: things stopped being really-hard and got medium-hard. We have an apartment with clean carpet and Venetian blinds; Mrs. Papadak, who lives below us on the sixth floor is usually sweet; and I'm mostly able not to think what flesh is capable of.

Hobb likes all the trees. I gave him a t-shirt from a boutique off campus that says Berzerkeley across the front. He laughed.

Hobb says we're normal. Looking at us, we could be anybody. I am sorting dirty clothes, Kate is reading Nancy Drew, and Willow's landed in front of the T.V. watching a commercial for douches. She sighs, turns from the filmed field of petals to Kate.

"Only dodos read Nancy Drew," Willow says.

"Get a life, fart-face," Kate answers, not moving her eyes from the book. "This is real. People don't die all the time. Someone gets bit by a black widow or trapped in a cave."

"No-huh."

"You think life is T.V. Your brain is barf."

"No-huh, you butt-hair."

"Dildo-face."

"Willow, Kate," I order, "help me." I hand Kate the Stain-Out-Spray. "Whites here," I tell Willow.

Willow holds her nose with her thumb and one finger, shaking her head no, her half-grown-out bangs dark, flapping over her eyes. She picks up a sock with her other thumb-tip and tosses it towards the couch.

I get turkey burger out of the ice-box for dinner.

"Gross," Willow yells, still plugging her nose. "Pray for your enemas."

"That is not what it says," Kate says low. "You are what you read, and you don't."

Willow picks up a pair of panties and holds them by the elastic on one finger. "Mom," she says, "Are these underwear white? I can't tell."

I don't answer. Willow throws them in the general direction of Kate.

"Mom," Willow pitches Sam's X-men shorts next to the love seat. "Can we do something? Go to the park? Go downstairs?"

The kids like running down the fire escape stairs to Mrs. Papadak's below us. Their footsteps make metal echoes. When we moved in Mrs. Papadak thought it was the second coming of Christ; that's how noisy it is when Sam plays Ghostbuster. Mrs. Papadak looks for signs from above, she told us; she's dying. It's what they sprayed here in the '60s, she said. She means old tear gas during riots.

Meanwhile, Mrs. Papadak raises baby birds for Feathers and Fins, which has outlets from Oakland to Walnut Creek. She tells stories of how there's money falling in smuggling birds, how in the Pacific Rim they stuff birds in toilet paper tubes and the tissues used too, in America. Lots of birds die, she says, but there's such a demand because most birds are too smart to breed in captivity.

Mrs. Papadak's place looks like a hospital unit for premature babies, incubators and tiny rag blankets and labeled bottles. My kids like to believe they help her out. Actually, Kate's pretty good at sticking the eyedroppers down the birds' throats and squeezing in seed-mush. She takes care they don't choke. The new ones are easy; without any feathers, you can see the lump of their meal drop down their gullet. When they get older Mrs. Papadak insists the food be followed with a finger, just to be safe.

"No," I tell Willow, "you're not going downstairs. No parks. I've got homework and Hobb is coming for dinner. He's picking Sam up from T-ball on the way here." I try to make my stomach unleash after I say this.

"Gross," Kate says.

"What is this!" Willow shrieks, girl-high. She aims my new pair of underpants and they drop in Kate's spread-eagle Nancy Drew pages.

Kate snatches them up, shakes out my panties. They look fragile, just a few strings. She sprays Stain-Out all over them, crushes them into a ball and hurls them at me.

I pick them up.

"Hey," I say. "They're not white."

"You're not decent," Kate says. "They're butt-floss."

"Set the table."

"You're sick. Hide those."

"The table."

"Don't you embarrass me, Mom."

"In front of who? Hide what? Masturbation? Who's in my life to humiliate you?"

"Who cares who?" Kate screams. "Sick-o. I hate you." Willow yells, like I'm not standing right there holding my panties, "I'm going down to see Mrs. Papadak." She runs out the door and Kate follows.

A long time ago, two years about—when Kate was eleven, Willow six, Sammy three—I took them to Price City Park in the middle of Utah. There were four skinny trees and lots of gray sand. I pushed Willow as long as she wanted on the chained swings and I climbed up the ladder of the rusty rocket ship slide and held Sammy between my legs and slid down. I told Kate she could take off her Keds—there was no glass in the sand—but she didn't. I asked her would she hold Sammy and keep Willow from standing up on the whirly-go-round. I grabbed the iron handles and pushed them, made it go as fast as I could. Kate sat in the middle of the circle of metal, her legs a knot around Sammy. Faster, Willow kept screaming: Make it faster, Mommy. So I held the bar with one hand and ran around and around, my other arm flapping, till I couldn't keep up anymore and had to let go and suck in burning air and watch my children whirling, that round metal disk spinning so fast all I could see were colors and blurs.

Sammy laughed. My hands smelled heavy, like kids' dirty hair. They wobbled, spun. Willow stood up and climbed on the handles as if she was riding a horse. My children rippled in the heat like a mirage.

There was a little girl crawling slowly to the swings. She had no legs. The bottom of her red sunsuit was sewed together where the holes used to be. She was twisting through the sand on her belly like half a lizard. Kate stood up. Sammy slopped off onto the hot sand and started to cry. Kate was leaning over the edge of the whirly-go-round, throwing up. Willow pointed her finger in front of my face. She shouted: Look at that, Mommy! What holds that girl's privates together?

A woman in purple pants stared at us. Her husband walked up. People, she said.

I said: Let's go.

I buckled Sam into the car and said: Seat belts, girls. Willow kneeled up in the back and pushed her face at the window.

She's pulling herself up the ladder, Willow told us.

We sat in the car.

See, I said. There are worse things. We've all got our legs.

They didn't answer.

I started the car.

Her daddy is with her, Willow said finally.


"Hi, Mommy."

Sammy is back from his T-ball. Hobb did pick him up. It's all right. Safe now. Sam is where I can see him. He butts his head into my stomach. "I'm starving to deaf."

"Hi," Hobb says. He's tall and he has dog-brown eyes. And Kate is right, his head is shaped like a lightbulb. He gives me a sort of hug and a pat and I'm scared he'll feel sweat from my skin through my shirt. He says, "Sam told me he has a girlfriend."

I say, "What?"

"She's in love with me, Mom. She wants to get married. We had sex today."

"What?"

"Sex. Where at rest time you climb on top of each other and make the matt wiggle."

"No. Sammy! My God!"

"And Hobb says when you burp with the guys you don't have to say pardon. Only with women."

"He's a great kid," Hobb says. Hobb knows the way to a woman's heart.

"Sammy, " I say. "Go. Run down and get Willow and Kate at Mrs. Papadak's. Tell them dinner."

He grabs up his G.I. Joe gun and is out the door, shooting.

Standing alone with Hobb, I can't think what to do. I forget, for a minute, how many kids I actually have. My mind spins view to view and I don't remember a way to seize one and believe it.

"Pardon me," I smile at him and get to the bathroom. Too much black feathers out from my eyes. Lip gloss. I stick panty shields in my shirt armpits to catch my sweat, so it won't show.

Back in the kitchen, I smile shiny at him. "Well. How was your day?"

Hobb laughs. He works from San Francisco, ferrying tourists to Alcatraz. I took the kids out one Saturday; that's how we met. I got sick from the boat and he gave me Dramamine. He let the girls play like they'd locked him in one of the prison cells.

He comes around behind me, puts his hands on my shoulders and molds his thumbs on my spine up to the base of my skull.

"Tense?" he asks.

The children are back.

"I'll eat if it's good," Willow says.

I've set the table myself, out on the metal-railed balcony. The sun is starting to sink. Dinner is pasta, turkey burger simmered with canned sauce, fruit cock-tail. Hobb brought a bottle of wine.

"How many bites do I have to have?" Sam asks.

"Delicious," Hobb says.

Willow glares. "We need a blessing," she says. "Our Father in Heaven," she starts, loud.

"This hurts my taste bugs," Sammy says after he spits out one spoonful.

Willow, eyes squished shut, sticks to her prayer: "Halloween be thy name."

"If you talk baby talk, I'm taking my dominoes back," Kate says.

"My king will come."

Sam gives his middle finger to Kate, holding the rest of his fingers curled down with his other stiff hand.

"He's already a pervert," Kate snorts.

"Children," I say.

Sammy gets off his chair and hides behind Hobb.

"Hobb," I say, "tell us about you. When you were a boy."

Hobb pulls Sammy onto his lap and takes a swallow of wine. "In the olden days, I was a little boy and I had a pair of cowboy boots. One day I got stuck in the mud in the pasture. I couldn't budge. I'd seen them pull cows out of that kind of mud with winches, and sometimes their cow legs stayed behind, stuck in the ground. I was scared. I cried till my daddy came. He pulled me out but those cowboy boots got sucked off my feet and stayed stuck. My dad tried to get them out but he couldn't with me under his arm. By next morning those boots were stuck forever. A scientist could dig them up like dinosaur bones. I planted pine nuts in them come summer."

"Are you aware," Kate says, "that every time you consume an alcoholic beverage you kill brain cells?"

"Yep," Hobb says and takes another drink. The wind ruffles his hair.

"Were you a real cowboy?" Sammy asks Hobb.

"Sort of. Except we had more sheep than cattle. I rode horses."

"The brain can't reproduce," Kate says. "You just get dumber."

"Now you take a horse, there's a dumb animal," Hobb says. "The smartest thing on a horse is the saddle. They're more trouble than kids; they tear fences down, tromp stuff up."

"I want a horse," Willow says.

"No, you should get something smart."

"Like what?"

"Pig. Pigs take care of themselves. Except when they're little they can't because the mama will roll over and crush her own babies."

"No way," Kate says. "Females don't kill their offspring. That's fathers, like fish and bears."

"Sometimes," Hobb says, "but some mothers do it. Rabbits, if they get stressed; and pigs too."

"I want a dog," Sammy says.

"Mom had a dog," Willow says. "Mommy, tell us a dog story."

"Gross," Kate announces.

"Which story?" I ask.

"Something with guns," Sam says. "Something with bad guys."

"I've got to clean up. It's past your bedtime."

The kids clear their plates when I ask. Sammy runs circles around the table and the iron core of the balcony reverberates. Hobb says he'll put Sammy down, and Willow and Kate escape clean-up, swearing they promised Mrs. Papadak they'd help her after dinner. She has new cockatiels.

Cleaning up?

It's not hard for just me and the kids. Hobb.

I remember thinking if I could get through the time being a cleaning woman I could get through any time. Maybe I could. Someone in Salt Lake must have knelt behind the groomed news-woman, scrubbing the blood on the sidewalk down to dull stains. Someone must have wondered about the feet in the future, walking over; it smoothed with dirt, gone, normal. But it wasn't me.

I scrape plates. The water is cold falling into the gargle of the garbage disposal. The glass glasses I got for tonight shine. I never used to use plastic. The meals I used to make took longer to cook than to eat, and I used serving dishes, not pans on the table. In the kitchen corner Kate had this big plastic horse mounted on springs with a dowel through its head. She'd hike up her nightie and bounce that horse back and forth, rocking and squeaking and staying right where she was. Katie would say: I want Daddy to put me to bed, and Willow would say: I want Daddy.

No one has memories that are real. We remember what we will, or can, or can't forget.

I go stand in the door of Sam's bedroom, the dishrag in my hand. Just to check, although I know what you see will play tricks.

Sammy has on his race-car pajamas, Ghostbuster goggles, his neutron pack strapped on his back. Hobb holds a toy six-shooter.

"I don't understand modern warfare," Hobb says.

"It's ghosts," Sam explains. "You have to get rid of them."

"Bedtime," I say. I watch Hobb dismantle the ghost-trap Sammy had rigged out of blocks. "Night-night," I say.

Sam wraps his arms around one of Hobb's legs and butts his head in Hobb's groin. "Bye, Hobb," he says.

This is normal, I think. This is what people all over Berkeley do when they turn off the T.V.

Hobb and I sit on the couch. There are wet stains under my armpits beyond where my panty shields stick.

"So," I say. "How's the bird-man of Alcatraz?"

He laughs. "I've escaped for tonight."

"I haven't," I say. "I've got lots of reading."

He is circling his hand on my knee cap. He starts walking his fingers inside my thigh like he's playing eensy spider.

"I have to look good for Miss Clairol." I mean I have to keep my grades up.

He lifts his hand from my leg.

"You want me to go?" he says.

"No." I say. This is true, but I say it as though it weren't.

"Well," he says, "I guess you can't let your roots show."

He gives me a kiss at the door, and I feel a chill under my breast bone, and I wonder if it was a good kiss or I imagined it. I need to see if Sam is asleep, check if he's breathing.

I am reading *Meteorites*. I think about the science professor with half a face. I wonder who can ever be sure what they saw in the sky. Then I hear screams.

Kate.

I crash out the door and run clumsily down the metal steps. Mrs. Papadak's backed to her balcony railing, her hands over her eyes. "Oh my God," she is saying.

Kate is still screaming.

Willow has her lips circled on a moist ball of pink skin. My legs are lost under me. "No," I yell at them all. "No," I keep yelling. Willow's mouth on a slick-blooded thing. I try to talk calm. "Tell me. Willow, you know you can tell me. What are you doing?"

Willow starts crying. "Mouth to mouth," she says. "But it's not working."

She holds out a wet-skinned membrane with black eyes and a beak.

"I can't do it," she says.

She kneels down on the floor, her dark hair falling over her hands and the dead chick. She rocks back and forth, crying.

Kate comes to me and buries her face in my neck. I feel the wet dead warmth of her on my flesh.

"It was the mama," Mrs. Papadak pulls her hands from her eyes. "Katie done a good job with the bitty, so she puts it down. So this mama just up throws it out of the nest. How could Kate see this? It falls on a heat bulb. No chance, dear God, nobody sees this. No chance."

"It's all right Kate," I say, stroking her head.

"I never seen a mama mistake that before," says Mrs. Papadak. "It's abnormality. This bitty not ready to fly."

By the time I get them upstairs Kate is silent. Willow shudders voiceless breaths in. Sammy is standing guard at our door. He points his He-Man-Laser straight at Kate's heart.

"I thought you were a ghost," he says.

I tell them all they can sleep in my bed and don't have to brush their teeth.

"Should we say a prayer?" Willow asks from the cold middle of my mattress.

Kate says, "Mom. Tell us a story, a true one." She puts a hand on Willow's knee. Sam squishes between the girls' legs.

I sit down on the edge of the bed. "When I was little," I say, "I had a dog." Their three brown heads almost touch.

"And she kept you from running out in the street . . . ," Willow prompts.

"And she'd open the gate and the doors with her mouth," Sammy says.

"And you'd have her for your head while you read and you'd scratch her tummy," Willow recites, "and she found her way home from when she got lost."

"She was a good dog," I say and lean over my bed to give each one a kiss.

"Mom," Kate says softly, "tell how she died."

"She got old," I say. "Her hips couldn't move, she had to crawl, she couldn't walk. She wouldn't eat."

"She was in pain," Kate says. "You'd see her hurt every time you looked in her eyes."

"She was old," I say, and Sam takes my hand.

"You let them put her to sleep," Willow says.

"Yes." I say. Sammy kisses my palm.

"You loved her that much," Kate says.

"Me too," says Sammy.

From old bedtimes come whispers, "If I die before I wake, I pray the Lord . . ." Kate, it is Kate reciting.

Willow's arms fold, her head down she sighs in, "my soul to take."

I say, "No."

"Our Father who art in Heaven," Kate says.

Sammy says, "A fart in Heaven?"

Willow is crying.

"Listen," I say to my children, "Look. No news is good news. We're all right. There are worse things. We're fine."

View after view after view. A balcony. A mother.
No chance?

This is my will: Not to remember. Not to look into
eyes. Not to believe in high places. Not to love.

# six

# CALLA LILIES

## *Jan Stucki*

One time before the sun came up, I heard her walking past. I heard the slow drag of her bullet-shot foot. And she hummed little pieces of songs. I knelt there in my garden with my two pairs of shears and I listened. I wanted to tell her that I got up early too. That I was the only early one in our neighborhood. I wanted to say that we—the early people—we shared the clean quiet of a settled place.

When I heard her, I could set the big ones on the ground, the branch clippers. But there were the little shears too. Small as scissors and sharp. If I left them in the piles of clippings, I might step on them. I might cut my own foot. And if I ran to the street to talk to her with shears in my hand—it was still dark—I couldn't surprise her like that, a woman alone.

The other thing we had in common was our children.

And later it occurred to me what I should have done. I should have cut some flowers for her. With my arms full of calla lilies at that hour I would have looked like one of the old señoras in the mercado. The ones you see in paintings. Seeing me with the calla lilies would have put her at ease. It would have reminded her of her home, of her children.

"I live by myself, too," is what I had said the day she moved onto our street alone. "I lost my children, too."

She had stood there, in her driveway, then finally said, "But this is North America. Who would kill them here?"

I asked her if she thought it was strange, that my children would choose to leave. That my children lived in London and Samoa and Mexico. And she said that one way or another they always leave you. They follow love, and if you see them alive again, their spirits are so broken they can hardly speak your name. If you see them again, is what she said.

My three girls. Just the day before I had tried to call up my daughter in Samoa. The operator had asked me to please try to not call on Sunday next time. If I could help it. She told me she could take the day off now and then if not so many people called on Sunday. And I never did get through to my daughter.

But see them again? My neighbor must have been able to tell. It must have shown like blood on my face.

That my girls did not want to see me again. I knew that she could tell.

I looked for her every morning in that early dampness. And when I heard the little bits of song, I was already waiting for her. I was crouching in my garden. Hands empty, shears over on the porch.

"Isabel," I said. "Isabel, it's me."

She stopped her humming and looked into the lemon tree. "It's me?" she said back. She looked behind her, too. To the sides.

"Don't be afraid, Isabel," I said, and I stood up this time. "I'm gardening." When she saw me, already reaching toward her with a handful of gardenias, she said, "It's you. Yes. I met you before."

She looked me in the eye, straight on, the way a strong mother would have, and she said, "Are you looking for me? Did somebody contact you?"

"About what?" I said. "It's so early and we're both awake." I did not understand her question just then. I tried to watch her eyes and not her hand. It was a pretty hand, prettier than mine, and she reached it to touch my gardenias, slowly. I drew them in closer to me until she was standing with both her feet in the soil of my garden. She stood her weight on the good foot.

I said, "See? Flowers." I told her about my gardenias. How I looked after them every day. How they weren't supposed to flower in this climate. And she was holding them with both her hands. If someone had passed by just then, if someone else in our neighborhood were awake at that hour, they would have seen us together. They would have thought we were friends.

I said, "What are those bits of songs you hum?" These were the songs of the revolution. These songs had followed her here. And when she said this, she looked carefully at me. She asked me what I knew about the revolution. And I was sorry. I didn't know enough. I didn't know what it meant that she—a woman with jeweled hands—would end up here.

Here the street was empty, but she kept looking down it. To make sure, she told me. A woman this careful. She must have been a good mother to her children. They must have trusted her.

She started to move back toward the street and I said, "Over here, the calla lilies." I had to show her the calla lilies. They were alongside the porch, all up and down it. I had to explain to her about them. I said she could sit on the porch dampness with me. She could be welcome here and we could wait for the sun to rise. If she wanted. There was a thermos of coffee already there. Two cups.

She asked me another question. She wanted to know if anyone had asked me about her. She said to please not mention this, about her being out early. It was her only time, she said. She let me pour the coffee and it spilled, three little drops on her wrist. Hot. So I dribbled it on my own fingers too. Little hot drops to find out what I had done to her. If I had scared her.

"I know this flower," she said. "I had this flower near my city. In the school where I taught." I told her that the strange thing was that when I got to my daughter's house in Mexico there were calla lilies planted all down the side of it. Along the wall, the way I had always had them. Like I had them at the house where she was born. The strange part was that my daughter could not have remembered that. I told my neighbor this. And she only nodded.

My neighbor was drinking her coffee standing up. It was not unkind, I guess, to stand when I sat. If she wanted to look around. She was looking at me, I thought. Her back to the street for the first time. But it was the shears she was watching. The small ones on the porch. My hand was on them and I had not known it. It was an accident, my own squeezing hand, and she had seen it. I slid them under my thigh. Out of her sight.

I told her that my daughter's house was long and narrow. That behind it, across this dusty driveway, there was a chicken coop. An enormous chicken coop. So many chickens you wanted to kick up the dust to keep from smelling them. I told her I had waited there for morning to come, for my daughter to come out in the yard and discover me. There were machines, too, and scales. My daughter owned all this.

"We didn't raise them on a farm," I told my neighbor. We raised them to think that chicken came from styrofoam plates at the grocery. My daughter had come out the door, though. She had said—the second thing she had said—was that it was time to give them their final shots before the slaughter. I could watch if I wanted to. She had called me "Mother."

Mother. She had brought me a glass of water to drink and said, "It's clean, Mother. It's okay to drink it." This daughter was the only one who had ever called me "Mama." Now, though, she was speaking to me in Spanish. Whole sentences. And then she would stop and say, "I'm sorry, Mother. English sounds so foreign to me now. I keep forgetting." She had only been there four years.

I did not mean to go on so long. My neighbor was sitting by then. She had sat down on my steps and she was watching me. Looking down sometimes at where the shears came from under my thigh. I had not wanted to tell this much. But I still had not gotten it right. I squeezed the handle in my fist to hide it.

But my neighbor still had to know this much. That I had not told my daughter I was coming.

When my daughter had come out of her house that morning, when she had seen me, the first words she had said were, "Mother, you should have told me. How long will you stay?" Then she had taken me to see her chicken coop. Little girls from the neighborhood had gathered inside it, eleven or twelve years old. Two of them were tying up a net and tossing all the chickens to one side of it. They were laughing, the little girls, and sometimes they started singing. My daughter sang too. Or she mouthed the words, at least.

But the word she said when she stepped into the chicken coop. It was just one word. A Spanish one. She said this and then nobody said another word aloud. Three of them would catch the chickens. Bring them to her. One would hold the chicken still in my daughter's lap. And my daughter stuck the needle in its thigh. Fast and sure. I had not taught her how to use a needle.

My daughter and these girls, they did this for two hours. Almost in silence. When she nodded, the girls knew what to do, what she meant. And when she nodded again, they knew what that meant too. She never looked up at me until they had finished.

By that time I had learned the brand names of all the old tires. That the calla lilies had forty-seven blossoms. I knew that on the scales I weighed fifty-eight kilos. And that the machine with the funnel propped over the spinning blades was where my daughter slaughtered the chickens with the drugged thighs.

My neighbor was still sitting, still watching me not watch her. She told me she had to be home before light. She told me she was sorry. I was sorry. I was the sorry one, I told her. It was okay. She could go now. I stood up, then I realized again what I should do. I should cut the calla lilies for her. Give some to her. Flowers to make her feel at home.

My neighbor looked to the street. To the car that was stopping there now. "Do you know that car?" she said. I had not seen it before. She said, "I'll wait a minute. Tell me some more." That was the end. There was no more to tell. Except that what happened was not my fault. My neighbor had to know that it was not my fault. And she asked what, what was not my fault.

I cut the stalk of a flower down and laid it across her lap. I told her that when the little girls had gone, that was when my daughter had finally invited me into her house. "We can eat now," she had said. "Alejandro is coming."

Even the dust could not have covered the smell of her then. Her hands were yellow. And all up her arms. It was all over her. Colored with bits of yellow or red. Bits of white and feathers. And she clamped one hand over the face of a fat chicken. A chicken with yellow serum in its thigh. This was my own daughter. She said, "In a minute, Mother, flip that switch there," and she stepped on the scale. My daughter, together with the big chicken, they weighed fifty-eight kilos. Just like me. I wanted to tell her this, that together they weighed the same as me and what did they make of that.

I said to my daughter, "Will it hurt? Does it know? I can become a vegetarian, you know." My daughter nodded to where the switch was. She slid that chicken down into the funnel. Head first. She held it by its feet, steady, sure.

I asked my neighbor if she had seen this before. The slaughter of chickens. If this happened in the mercado, next to the stacks of bananas. She said, "Yes. It was like that. If that's what you think." I was filling her lap with flowers.

For me, there had always been pavement, I told her. Always something between me and blood. But there the ground around the machine was stained dark. And my daughter, with her yellow hands, was nodding at the switch. "It's going to be okay, Mother," she said. The chicken in the funnel was not moving and I wanted my daughter to leave it there and move this switch for me. She looked so tired, so dirty. She kept watching the chicken.

So I moved it just a little. I was going to turn it on fast and then turn it off. I was going to get it over with. I moved the switch just barely. Just enough. Almost enough. The screeching came from the blade first. Or from the chicken maybe. I heard it before I screamed myself. I was not the first one. The thud of the table was next. The scrambling, kicking chicken feet, everything moving chaos except the stuck blade.

It jammed, my daughter said, from my switching not quite enough. The blades, I guess they turned enough to stop it from screaming. But not from kicking. I don't know. They stuck, I think. Stuck half way into its neck. Enough so that I could hear the blood start to splatter in the bucket. So that I felt a splash of wet hit my knees under the table. My daughter pushed me away. She switched it up and down up and down. That chicken there kicking and bleeding and kicking. And she pounded on the table until the blades unstuck. I don't know if it was five seconds or five minutes. I don't know. I kept saying, "I'm not like that anymore. I'm better now." I wanted my daughter to see that I'm not like I used to be.

My flowers were cut. My calla lilies were all in a pile. All stacked in a pile in her lap. I had not meant to cut them all. I had said too much. I had scared my new neighbor already. And there was no place to set my shears again. My daughter could have flipped the switch to start with.

It was light already. My neighbor was watching that car. She said to me, "Your flowers. What have you done?" But she was watching that car still. And when it started up, when it drove past with a woman driving it, my neighbor stood. She set my calla lilies beside her and said, "Your flowers." And she said, "Thank you."

The flowers were for my neighbor, though. I gathered them, took them all in my arms. And I followed her out to the street, her uneven steps. "Here," I said. I put the flowers in her arms again. "Take these. All of them."

She took them without slowing down. "Thank you," she said. "It's time I have to go. Thank you." And she moved back into the street. And I stood in my drive and watched her. Her carrying my flowers, safe in our neighborhood, and pulling her one shot foot behind her.

# seven

# BLUE, BLUE, MY LOVE IS BLUE

*Pauline Mortensen*

All my life, all I ever wanted to do was dance. From the time I first climbed out on the kitchen table and turned on my heel to dance a late-night tango for my little sisters, a late-night tango clicking across the table top and tapping my way out of their world into another, from that time I knew. To the time of my senior prom when I held Carl Banner under the crepe-paper moon and nudged him through all that we had practiced in the church gym, nudged him and tried to hold forever the feeling that always came when the lights went dim, tried to hold him with the last dance tune that I hummed in his ear, "Blue, Blue, My Love is Blue," which I hoped would settle in there like cement. Even then I knew. For all that time, and all the time before and since, all I ever wanted to do, me, Lena Laviston, all I ever wanted to do was dance.

But when I was ten, a child of ten, capering around

the kitchen in my stocking feet, bidding for attention, my father leaned back in his dinette chair from where he was bidding at cards and said, "Get the hell out of here while I'm shooting the moon." It was an early reflection on my talent, that it was doomed to be misperceived, flung aside like so many countless nines. It was a stunning blow, and the shock of it rolls over me still, when I think of how my socks would sing on the kitchen tile. But on I danced, in closets, in corners, across all their lives, even though I was threatened with "No more new socks." No more new socks until I learned to appreciate the ones I had. No more new socks until I stopped acting like a fool and did the dishes like I was told.

But still I danced, on stages made of beds or under the spotlight on the kitchen dinette. And I danced around in my own little talent shows, my own little dress rehearsals, with my sisters as audience, and hoped that someday I would be discovered.

Because I always knew that I would be one of the few. Even as far back as I can remember, before all my sisters came along, and my father would lift me by the arms, his first born, and glide my bare feet on the tops of his rough shoes, and he would swing me away and away to the beautiful Tennessee Waltz. Even then I think I knew, being lifted, as I was and twirled by my arms in glory, all the way up to his chest.

I never let anything else creep in. Just dancing. There were little lace tutus for the Primary Parade, starched bonnets at Easter Pageant, and angel wings and tights for Christmas plays. It was all there in me from the beginning. It's important to get the facts straight. Because I didn't take up dancing in high school just to get out of the house. I didn't do it for that. With me it was a gift that I had to use. With me, it was natural.

And this is where it's got me. Me, sitting here listening to my sister Lucky tell me about her love life in Helena, Montana, this guy she's been living with hot-and-cold for the last five years. I mean, I'm sitting here grinding peas through the top of the Magic Food Mill and feeding the mess to the baby. I'm working my sixth child onto solid food and off my breast, and Lucky's sitting there in her denim halter top with half an acre of breast resting on my kitchen table, and she's telling me how Stan, that's the guy's name, likes to give *her* a good suck. If I know what she means. I could have lived without knowing that, but she tells me anyway.

She tells me everything I don't want to know, and I can't tell her anything. That's Lucky. Always trying to catch up and prove something to the world. To listen to her talk, you'd think she invented it. My parents called her Lucky because when she was born the cord was twisted around her neck, and she untwisted herself right at the last minute and came out okay, and I always thought she turned a second too late and cut off the air she had to think with.

Anyway, that was us back then. Lena, Lucy, Lucky,

Lorna, and Lark. Five little clones whose names people would sing out like a jingle until they came to the right one. Five little clone girls dressed in Easter bonnets and one long name. That was us—the girls—sticking to the back seat of our father's '57 Rambler and hoping, each one of us, that we wouldn't scrape our legs on the metal catch along the front of the seat, or get popped in the head before we got to Sunday School.

So my little sister, the one we all teased because she was fat, she says to me that she likes to try new things. Her and Stan aren't afraid of trying new things, if you know what she means.

And I say, "Lucky. Does this guy love you or what?"

And she says, "Yes. Oh, yes. He likes to do it three or four times a day."

"But Lucky," I try to clear this up. "Does he want to marry you or anything?"

And she says, "Well, if that's not love, I don't know what is." And she stops there because she knows now about my recent divorce and pretends she doesn't want to rub anything in.

The baby squirms sideways and nearly wrenches out of my arm I got clamped around her middle. Lucky says, "Little yahoo, little bugger," and I pull tighter with my forearm so I won't lose my grip on the Magic Food Mill in my hand.

And here's the thing about Lucky, the thing everyone knew about her all her life while she was growing up at home—Lucky and her "piano talent." Lucky signing up for the talent assembly, her name on the bulletin board in the hall in front of third grade. A little black smudge mark under her name. A little of Lucky on the board for everyone to see. The "professional" Lucky. And us other kids, her sisters, shrinking into corners when anybody asked, "What's this about Lucky?" Me and Lorna walking just a little bit ahead all the way home because we knew the secret about Lucky—Lucky plunking away at home with two fingers, never-had-a-lesson-in-her-life Lucky. Because it was bound to rub off on us, see. No matter how it would turn out, it was bound to rub off. Lucky getting up on stage and plunking out "Old McDonald" or "Dolly Dear." Or Lucky not getting up on stage, making some excuse at the last minute so that everyone would groan with recognition of the old tale of our infamy. Our family shame that seemed to have no end and no beginning. That Lucky should think of doing this made our social rise all the more impossible. Lucky and her piano talent. Just like all the Lavistons.

But nobody knew about me. I was the real thing. I could dance. Knew it when I swung my hips, every time I went out to get the mail. Knew it when I walked up the junior high stairs with a bunch of junior high boys behind. Knew it when I danced with myself in the dark to the totally delectable tune of "Chantilly Lace, a pretty face, a ponytail hanging down." Knew it when there wasn't a soul around or a drift of music in the air. Even then I knew. I just knew.

But here I am and Lucky says, "In my mind, we're married. A common-law marriage. He hangs his pants on the bedpost just the same. Sometimes his place, sometimes mine. It's all just the same. In my mind, we're married."

In my mind, she is something else. And now I have to ask myself this: What choice did I have being born into such a family? After high school graduation, my father gave me two choices. I could stay home and help build the new barn, or I could go to a business school, a one-year mill, and pay my own way. He had too many daughters coming along for anyone to get any fancy ideas about college. And I was the first one. I had to set the example. And when it was Lucky's turn to leave home, she got to go to state four years and now she waits tables.

I had to go into business because that was where the money was. I couldn't believe they tried to teach me shorthand when all my talent was in my feet, tried to give me dictation when my spirit was free, tried to cram office machines down my throat when I was light as a feather. I couldn't believe one word anyone ever said to me until I discovered the weekend dance at the Ridgeway and Freddy Street dancing to "Hey Jude," strumming his stomach like it was a guitar.

I always was a sucker for a slow dance tune, something that gave you goose bumps. Give me a two-step or a fox trot any day. Something where your partner takes you in his arms and waltzes you out of this world into the next.

So anyway, I'm sitting here listening to Lucky, The Pianist, because, hey, I figure I've had six kids, that's one less than my mother, and I figure there isn't much Lucky can tell me about sex. I figure maybe after awhile she will slow down and ask *me* a question. I mean I have had six children pulled from my groin, six times split open by the cry of new life, six times I have multiplied and fulfilled the measure of my creation and I think I know something she doesn't. But does she slow down and listen to me?

I mean I could tell her a little bit about life in general. Not just sex. About how people say things about having so many kids. Like I'm some kind of nymphomaniac to have had so many. Like I can't control myself. You can't tell me I don't know what they say behind my back about me and Freddy. Me and Freddy, the fertility twins. Freddy didn't mean for things to turn out the way they did. Things just happened. But me, I wanted those babies, every one. Every one was a little bit special. A little shaving off the soul of God. And my only regret is that Freddy took off before I had any more. And that's what I tell those people who think they know so much about my life. Who like to stick their noses in where they don't belong. Because if there's anything I can't stand, it's people wanting to know your business and run your life for you, just to get a thrill, and who have no intentions of sticking around long enough to help out. And me on welfare, a divorced woman without an education, trying to raise six hungry kids. If they don't want to help us out, they can just mind their own business.

Anyway, I heard that kind of crap all my life, about people who have more kids than they can afford. Like it wasn't the Lord's commandment or something. They stick it to you in little ways, like when you are getting out of the car at the wholesale grocery. You are unloading from the Rambler, just coming out into the fresh air, when someone says something about a pack of circus clowns climbing out of a Volkswagen. Makes you feel like dirt. And then there is always someone getting you mixed up with one of your sisters, which they think is funny. I could tell Lucky all this, but she should know about humiliation being fat. Six kids and I still have a better figure.

In fact, I could tell her some stories about Freddy, but why bother. He's history. A faded tune on the dance floor. Some double-timing hot-step from the 1960s that no one even wants to remember.

Lucky gets up to get a drink of water. There is a lull in the drone that has been pounding in my head ever since she arrived. Like closing up the piano after the kids' hammering. Like the first day of school after they've gone. Like valium. All this talking and talking about Stan and his horny self. Lucky takes a long swig at the sink and then comes back and sets the plastic glass onto the wood table I sanded myself. A water moustache purses on her upper lip, which she has no intention of wiping dry. She has been revived. So her and Stan like to try new things, she says. Like she hasn't mentioned this before. They like to try new positions, if I know what she means. For instance, she says. And she shows me with her hands. Meanwhile, I'm wiping Georgette's mouth, and trying to keep a straight face. Because it is hard for me to imagine anyone straddling Lucky in any position. Lucky on the top. Lucky on the bottom. If there is a God in heaven, you'd think He'd spare me this. After all I've done to build up the kingdom, having my kids and all. But no. I have to listen to every word. This is my sister who I haven't seen in five years, and she is a guest in my house. She can gesture with her hands all she wants and draw diagrams on the table. This is my sister. Which way do I like it best, she says. Which way did I like it best with Freddy? And now she has me. She wants me to diagram back. He was fast Freddy, all right. But to Lucky I say, "Some things are sacred."

And that cuts her off a little. She takes another drink. There is a hand calculator on the table where I have been adding up the check book. Although why I try to balance it, I'll never know. A divorced woman is a hopeless case. And Lucky is picking up the calculator and punching in some numbers. "Let's see. You figure seven-point-five times a week, fifty-two weeks out of the year, minus a few months when we're not living together, times five years and you come up with something like this." She shows me the figure. I do my best to ignore it, but it's big. Real big.

Georgette spits peas down my blouse, and I hit her in the mouth with the burp rag. All my life I never minded kids. I was the oldest. I had my hands full with all the babies at home. All my father's babies, born one after the other until there were six of us, and then bingo, there he finally was—the boy, little Bernie. My baby brother, the little live-wire we had all been waiting for, the reward after the long parade of girls, after trial and error, after "Slam—bam—thank you, Ma'am." This is the way Lucky always described it about our father—the way he did it to Mother. The way any man will get away with if he can.

And how does she know so many stupid things? How does she know so many things that passed right over my head while we were growing up? How could she know such a thing about our parents? And now she's talking about coming. How many times, she wants to know. How many times in one night? But she doesn't wait for an answer. "Some things are sacred, I know," she says, and holds up her hands to spare herself.

Then she drops both hands on the table flat. "You do come, don't you?"

And I say, "Of course, I do. Where'd you think this one came from." And I point my chin at Georgette. And then I listen to what she has to say next. About how when we were kids and liked to climb up the flag pole. That's kind of what it feels like, she says. The way it feels when you have your legs wrapped around double, your toes locked behind your ankles, and you slide down fast from the top. "Yeah, I know," I say.

But I never was much of a climber. Lucky was the one who always made it to the top. I'm getting this picture of it all in my head. Lucky, all alone out on the playground at school, going up and down the flagpole. Lucky, all alone under the covers in the bedroom at home where six girls slept. And Lucky and Stan irretrievably tangled, arms and legs intertwined, in some waterbed with mirrors over there in Montana. And then there is me, me and Freddy. But Lucky is ahead of me.

"Everybody knew why you came home from business school," she is saying. "Everybody knew it was because of you and Freddy, because of sex."

"Who is everybody?" I am saying. "What gave you that idea?" I see me now coming home in disgrace, a failure at typing, a failure at dictation. Barely passing office machines. "What do you mean everybody knew it was because of sex?"

"Well, that is what Fran told me," says Lucky. Fran is our cousin who married an accountant and who has enough money to take one of my kids but has never offered. And Lucky says, "Fran said that Mom took you to the doctor when you got back to see if you were pregnant, because the old lady you were staying with said you were out late all the time. She says you catted around all hours of the night and she had no control over you, and if Mom and Dad didn't get you home soon, you'd be pregnant. And Mom took you to the doctor, and he said you didn't bleed, and that's why Freddy Street followed you up here after you left school, and you got married so fast." And Lucky leans back, looking satisfied with herself.

I mull over what she has said to me, and then suddenly it is like the room has changed color. So that's what all that was about. The doctor looking up between my legs. Because I needed a physical, my mother said, but really because they never understood. Nobody understood. About how I had this special talent, how I had to go to those dances at the Ridgeway or die. Trapped as I was in downtown Boise. And now Lucky is telling me this after all these years, stuff she has known all along. Stuff everyone has been saying behind my back all along. Here I am a mother in Zion and people have been saying things like that. People been knowing things that I didn't know myself—why my parents kicked me out. Why they don't even look at my kids. And now I see it all. The reasons for things over all these years. The way they have been seeing my whole life for the last fifteen years, my marriage, my children, my divorce, and all my bad luck. Everything's upside down. They think the Lord's against me because of the way I've lived, and I'm getting exactly what I deserve for being somebody I never was.

I let Lucky rattle on for one more sentence, something about Amos being early, and then I let her have it. And this is what I say. "The only reason there's a divorce in this family is because as it turns out my husband is homosexual. And the one thing I won't stand for is people thinking that everything has been my fault. And the one thing you better get straight right now is that I don't enjoy it in any position, not up or down, not regular or otherwise. And the real reason I'm mad is this: All my life I've been good. I went to church and took my sisters when my parents said to go. I put up with little Bernie kicking me on the shins and didn't hit him back like I wanted. And I even went away to the school where father said I had to go. And what did I get for doing what I was told? I got religious and I got shin splints. I got a bad report card and I got kicked out of the house. And now what it comes down to is this: I have a husband who enjoys sleeping with men better than me and has no intention of paying child support, and I've got to feed my kids on a crummy paper route. And not one relative will lift a finger to help. Not my sisters who have problems of their own. Not my cousin, who thinks she's Hedda Hopper. Not my father or my mother, because they think I'm the whore of Babylon."

And that's what I tell Lucky more or less, sitting there across from me with her mouth hanging open. Words like that coming from me, I suppose. Well, I let it sink in for about two minutes, and then I tell her to get the hell out.

So they have these dances out at the Cotton Club on Highway 95. It's a bar, but a real nice place. Live music and dancing. It says so on the sign. And you don't think I'll fit in, but time will tell. As soon as the sitter gets here, that's where I'm headed. Because I'm still young. I can still swing my hips. Maybe I will be rusty a little at first, maybe I'll gasp for breath the first time around. But I think I'll make it. Because once you've seen the ceiling whirling away, you never forget it. It's always in your body somewhere. You are always, from that time forward, one with the dance. And maybe I won't find him on the first try, maybe not even on the second. But I will find him. Some man. Some dancing man who will be good for more than one time around the dance floor. Some man standing there along the side in the blue dim light, waiting—waiting for me to step out into my slow sway, in my velveteen plush dress, some man waiting somewhere, who still knows how to dip.

eight

# FINDING A WIFE FOR MY BROTHER

*Helen Walker Jones*

I'm dancing with a navigator, and when he invokes patriotism I don't tell him about my distinguished American heritage. I keep my mouth shut but go on thinking of a bumper sticker I saw once: America was Built on the Blood of Indians. It was pasted to the rusted chrome of a '69 Ford Galaxie, powder blue–the blue of wildflowers in March on the reservation and the color of half the houses. In the Galaxie were six men–three in front, three in back, each as big as a fullback–decked out in Stetsons with peahen feathers in the hatbands.

Thinking of that car, I press my mouth to this boy's ear, he bends to me, and I whisper: "How come Crazy Horse and Sitting Bull only brought a few hundred warriors to fight Custer?" When he gives up, I tell him, "They could only get two cars."

I grew up hearing these jokes. I laughed. My brother didn't. He developed what is known as a social conscience. My sibling, James Madison Waxwing—named for the fourth president of the United States—lives on the reservation by choice and spends every weekend presiding over Tribal Alcoholism Encounters. This sounds like a booze party; it's actually a bunch of guys lounging on metal folding chairs, nodding off while Jim tells them that only a higher power can save them from drink.

Jim's nine-to-five job consists of sitting in front of the cracker barrel with the old gents, smoking and chewing, his chair tilted back on two legs. He's the psychobabble king of eastern Montana, and for this he's paid an enormous salary, drives a government Ford with black-wall tires, and sleeps in an absolutely free house, even if it is painted turquoise with red woodwork. His official title is Substance Abuse Counselor.

He's the reason I'm down here now at the Co-Pilot Lounge. Jim is back at my apartment consummating his latest conquest. My roommate, Bonnie, is the lucky girl.

Barefoot on the shellacked dance floor of the Co-Pilot is not where you would find me on a typical Monday night, but here I am. My shoes kicked off, I'm swaying in duplicate with this boy ten years my junior, running my palms over his buzz-cut while he tells me "America, the Beautiful" was written in Colorado Springs, home of his alma mater, the Air Force Academy. One day this boy hopes to get shot down over Vladivostock in a super-secret ebony jet so that he can use his junior high Russian and get his name in the papers. Maybe even die for his country. "I was trained to be a hero," he tells me. I don't mention that my brother was a conscientious objector and that he still wears his hair in a waist-length braid.

For a while in the seventies, Jim even played at being a hero out of James Fenimore Cooper, wearing beaded shirts and a quiver of arrows, no less, while he wrote fan letters to Marlon Brando for his advocacy of Native American rights. That year, after Jim dumped one of my fellow nursing students, she told everyone that he had picketed the priest's house, burned Bibles at the Custer Burial Grounds, and demanded that she indulge in perverse sex. I can personally verify the first two, so I was inclined to believe the third. Still, I'd never mention this to one of the boys at the airbase who thinks it's quaint that I can do the hully-gully.

These fly-boys have a fervent belief in machismo. "Hands-on" is a favorite phrase in their training manuals and innate in their philosophies, too. My brother, on the other hand, favors the long-distance approach. While I'm at work, he romances my roommate over the phone, tenderizing her for his in-the-flesh visits. I'm talking about this like it's soon to come, like he isn't back there right now, dazzling her with his pecs and humbly confessing that he was the first Ph.D. ever to come out of Rosebud, Montana.

Every Sunday for the past eight weeks, he's been on the phone, asking in his husky voice, "Bonnie, are you as cute as my sister says you are? I hear nurses give great backrubs. I can't wait to find out." His low-key occupation—interacting with the brothers on the rez—leaves him too much free time to chase women, like Bonnie Gardner.

The first time I ever saw Bonnie, she was pushing an I.V. pole down the hall of the labor-and-delivery unit, yelling, "Out of my way. This woman's about to pop out her eighth kid." Bonnie was wearing purple running shoes and, in place of surgical greens, a shiny white jumpsuit that appeared to be made of parachute material. She stared at me and said, with a grin, "I hope they let me throw the placenta into the garbage."

Later that day, I saw her again in the nurses' locker room. She squinted at my nametag as she tucked her bushy reddish hair into a bun. "Veronica Waxwing," she said. "Is that your stage name, or what?" She said the basement rooms were the coolest and told me about the vacancy in hers. Ten minutes later she showed me a plastic card in her wallet that said: Believe it or not, Florence Nightingale is not dead. It had a picture of Bonnie on the left, just like a driver's license.

I had known her two months before Jim started his Sunday phone crusade, catching her between shifts to inquire about her health, her sex life, and her orange Thunderbird. He probably did a questionnaire on her drinking, too. Anyway, she was frantic to meet him and, this afternoon, just before his flight arrived, she stumbled through the basement door, dressed in her scrub suit, and slumped into the chair across the table from me. "Tip that granola this way," she said, reaching into the box for a handful. We never cook.

"Was it hot in the delivery room?" I asked her.

"Slightly," she said. "But we delivered a nine-pound boy and the mama didn't hemorrhage a speck." She walked to the fridge and peered in at our leftovers. I imagined them, furred with mold. Sir Alexander Fleming would be proud. "Eggs and milk," she said. "That's it. Are we going to cook for your brother?"

"Go ahead," I said. She piled her hair over the left ear and let it fall.

"Men," she said. "There was a new government doc there today. 'What do I do next, nurse?' he asks me. So I delivered the baby while he stood in the corner." Bonnie wiped her forehead with the back of her wrist, reminding me of the way ladies try out perfume at the cosmetics counter. "I could use a glass of lemonade," she said, "or your brother to blow cold air on my insteps." She propped her feet on the kitchen table, next to the rattan fruit basket, her bare toe just brushing an apple. "I can't wait to see him," she said. "Maybe he'll model his loin cloth for me."

"Don't count on it," I said, thinking of Burt Lancaster movies in the church hall on the rez, where the people cheered for the cavalry during the bloody skirmishes.

Jim took a taxi from the airport and settled his fake alligator suitcase inside the door of our apartment, announcing, "I'm here, ladies. Come and get me." Bonnie demurely pulled up her knee socks and smiled with just the corners of her mouth.

He kissed her lightly on the cheek and stroked her hair. Leave 'em hungry is his motto. He wanted to go sight-seeing, on foot. The three of us strode down the wide sidewalk with Jim in the middle. Bonnie and I kept batting the mosquitos from our legs. I let them walk ahead, and watched her rusty-colored hair bouncing across her shoulder blades, his braid swinging from side to side. There is a legend about a warrior tying a beaver pelt to his head as he swam a river dusted with ice. In the cold, damp air, the beaver's tail supposedly stuck to the warrior's neck, like a wet tongue to metal. And that became his braid.

The bells were chiming at St. Andrew's and a chubby old woman emerged from her front door, knotting a black scarf among the folds of her chin. I thought of the white clapboard church on the reservation, its wooden cross silhouetted against cirrus clouds, the outhouse off to the side like a whitewashed penitent rising to bear witness.

"Pretty girls," a drunk in an airman's cap muttered, reaching out to stroke my butt as he passed us.

"Aha," Jim said, shaking his head. "And you two claimed you'd been living like nuns."

"The closest I've come to a penis was an article I read on catheter care," Bonnie said. Jim laughed and slipped his arm around her shoulder. I wanted to tell him nurses talked like that, but it didn't necessarily mean anything. "We could've had our pick of the cowboys," Bonnie continued, "but they like their women natural." She stabbed her armpit with her fingertips. Jim grinned and ran his hand over the thick base of his braid.

While Bonnie and I made a salad, Jim sat on the couch, smoking and watching a cop movie with the volume turned off. That way he could hear the jets taking off. "Man, it must be great, living next to an airbase," he said. "I might have gone in the service if they could have guaranteed me a jet."

"At one time I wanted to marry a pilot," Bonnie said.

Jim ignored this invitation to explore her past. "This place is as bad as a reservation house," he said, reaching behind the couch to touch the yellow walls stained with fingerprints.

"Hey," Bonnie said, "I want to hear about the time you were arrested. What was it like in the slammer?"

"Veronica's been spinning tall tales," Jim said. "It was just a few hours in the county jail."

"Don't lie," I said. "She knows all about you."

"Well, Bonnie," Jim said, standing and fishing a matchbook from deep in his pocket, "if you want to hear some authentic Indian lore, come on over here." She snuggled beside him on the couch and watched as he built a fire of scrap paper in a big glass ashtray on the coffee table. "This," he said, "is an altar to Buffalo Woman. She controls the elements."

"Great," Bonnie said. "Let's pray for snow."

"Okay," Jim said, stretching out on his back, lowering his head and shoulders to the linoleum, his arms rigid at his sides, his eyes closed. "Quiet now," he said. "I'm invoking the old lady's spirit."

"This is fabulous," Bonnie whispered, glancing over at me to see if he might be serious. "I feel like I'm in the Black Hills and here come some Apaches in warpaint."

Jim corrected her without opening his eyes. "There were no Apache in the Black Hills," he said. "Shoshone."

"Then you're a Shoshone warrior," Bonnie said. She reached down and set her palm flat against his chest. "I would love to bear at least nine children before I pack it in and get buried in my buffalo-hide shroud," she said.

The corners of Jim's mouth turned up. I was feeling like a voyeur, so I escaped to the bathroom to wash my face. As I turned the doorknob, I heard Jim say to her, "You're gorgeous, Grey Eyes."

When I came out, they were both sitting on the floor,

Jim with his back to me, his dark braid brushing the top of his leather-tooled belt. "So answer me this," she was saying. "Are you, or are you not, a real, honest-to-God Indian?"

"I'm three-quarters Indian," Jim said. "But I tell people my father was a wild warrior. Actually, I never saw my father, except in his picture on the piano."

"How sad," Bonnie said. "Veronica never told me that. What did he look like?"

"He looked like Jim," I said. "But without the braid."

Bonnie scooted closer to him on the linoleum. "How come you never saw him?"

"He ran off," Jim said. "Our mom was nineteen and pregnant."

"With me," I said. "Jim was a year old."

"What did he do for a living?" she wondered.

"He fixed school buses," Jim said. I couldn't believe he was telling her this. Her father, after all, was a board-certified neurosurgeon. "From what I heard, he was sort of an incompetent mechanic," Jim went on, unwrapping a candy bar. He took a bite, then held it in front of Bonnie's face until she bit some off. Nuts and chocolate stuck to her front teeth. Jim sat on the arm of my chair. He shook one leg from the knee down, like a sprinter warming up. "I get these charley horses," he said. "Must be sexual tension."'

"All the guys in this town are twenty-three years old and just out of flight school."

FINDING A WIFE FOR MY BROTHER / 121

"Too young to appreciate age and experience," Jim said. "A woman's not ready till she's on the backside of thirty," he said, opening his suitcase and holding up a rectangular white box. Bonnie took off the lid, spread tissue paper over the sides and said, "Is this authentic?" It was a moldy-looking buckskin shirt with yellow beads forming chevrons across the chest. "You bet," he said. "An old guy named Tom Meltingtallow gave it to me. A nice guy, really, once we got him on methadone."

"You have interesting friends," Bonnie said.

"See these?" Jim went on. "These are porcupine quills. The shirt's nearly a hundred years old."

That night at the hospital I had three quick deliveries in a row and showed one of the mothers how to press in just above her nipple so the baby could breathe as it nursed. The stretch marks slanting into her pubic hair reminded me of the chevron shirt and the stripes on her husband's uniform. As I waited for the placenta, I thought of Jim's hair fanned over Bonnie's lavender eyelet pillowcase, the symbol of his unbound humility and submission. He had told Bonnie things he had never told any other woman, as far as I knew; and I wondered, right then, what Bonnie would do if she married him. After a society wedding in Walnut Creek, she could move back to the rez, sitting with her argyles resting on the cracker barrel, rousing herself occasionally to dispense a dose of methadone. Or maybe she could work weekends at the tavern out on Highway 57 dressed in a buckskin G-string and pasties, billing herself as Minnehaha.

In the nurses' locker room, I slipped into my jeans and red silk blouse. The three-to-eleven shift was just ending and a group of orderlies and nurses was heading to the Co-Pilot. "Come on, Veronica," one of them shouted from the wash basin. "There are terrific men down there. Smooth-faced as nectarines."

"Let's practice our Kegels before we go, girls," someone shouted from the other side of the lockers. "Tighten, relax, tighten, relax. I do them faithfully at every stoplight."

I didn't feel like going to the Co-Pilot. It was late and I was tired. Jim and Bonnie had already had two hours to themselves. I figured that was sufficient. But when I walked through the basement door into our dingy apartment, I heard the shower running through the bathroom wall. Jim was standing naked in the front room, a beer can in his hand, his thick black hair was spread loosely over his shoulders, just as I had pictured it on Bonnie's pillowslip. "Hey, Sis," he said, taking a swig of beer, making no attempt to cover himself, "she's not bad. Red pubic hair. I like that."

Looking at him, I thought of only one word: underbelly. "It's about time you liked somebody," I said. And I stood there, looking at the notch in his earlobe (the result of a human bite acquired in a bar brawl), embarrassed at seeing him standing there, brazenly sweating, though the air in the room seemed suddenly cool. I stepped back through the door and shut it, stroking the worn metal knob, remembering Jim's reservation house where the neighbors in their tar-paper shacks beat each other's heads against the wall, between listening to Johnny Cash records.

I drove to the Co-Pilot Lounge, making all the stop-lights, and slid into a big red booth. The burly blond guy in the Pike's Peak sweatshirt asked me to dance and I ignored the age difference and interlocked my fingers at the base of his skull, pressing my breasts up against the insignia on his shirt.

He talked about Colorado Springs and his desire to become a hero and, when I asked him if he knew that America was built on the blood of Indians, he focused intently on my cheekbones and said, "I think they prefer to be called 'Native Americans.'"

Then he laughed and spun me around on one foot, and for a while I forgot about Bonnie Gardner at home in the shower, trying to scrub herself clean enough to suit my brother's taste.

nine

# THE WAY I LIVE

*Patricia McConnel*

[for Katharine Coles]

My mother doesn't understand the way I live. Every time she comes to visit she says, "Miriam, I don't understand the way you choose to live your life." She doesn't emphasize the word "choose" but I hear the emphasis anyway. Well, I tell you.

"Mim," I say (my mother's name is Miriam, too, Mim for short), "I live like I want to live and just because you don't understand it doesn't mean it's wrong."

I was born in the thirties, which was a bad time for everybody but it was especially bad for women. My mother was seventeen and if it wasn't for the fact that she had to leave Virginia because she was pregnant with me she might never have gone to Las Vegas and become a show girl. She was that gorgeous. But anyway she named me Miriam Jr., just like a

125

boy, which of course has been a source of embarrassment to me my entire life. Cute, she thought it was. She was only seventeen. As soon as I came of age I changed my name to Suzanne but Mim still calls me Miriam, which is bad enough, but when she wants to make me *really* mad she calls me Junior.

Growing up in Las Vegas is not what you may think. I didn't know there was anything unusual about my childhood. I slept while my mother was working. She kept me in a bassinet backstage when I was little and then when I was a toddler I slept on a couch in her dressing room. What I'm saying is, I slept through anything that might have given me wild ideas. I have vivid memories of being carried to the car in the dead of night, half-asleep, when Mim's last show was over, and seeing all the colored, flashing lights reflected in the geyser fountains, and thinking I was in the Land of Oz. I loved it.

I never lost my love of glitter and bright lights. Years later, when I worked at the casinos, I liked to walk through the clubs and hear the constant clink of coins as the slots paid off. I liked the black mirrors on the walls and the red carpets and the wonderfully garish crystal chandeliers, all giving this illusion of posh elegance. It remained my personal Oz, and I never gambled. Most casino employees don't. But daughter of a show girl that I am, I still love dresses with sequins and rhinestones and feathers—the more the better—and green snakeskin cowboy boots, and earrings that light up. I once had a sweat shirt with a slot machine on the front with gold-colored metal and colored glass stones and little tiny lights that went on and off like the slot was paying off—there were little batteries on the back I had to take off every time I had it cleaned. Imagine, a sweat shirt that had to be dry cleaned. Only in Las Vegas. I loved that sweat shirt. Tacky, but I can't help it. Of course, the way I live now, I don't have much occasion to wear that kind of thing.

Mim shared apartments with other show girls and one of them would usually be between shows and would pay her share of the rent by taking care of me while my mother slept in the daytime. I thought these women were my aunties. I was seven or eight years old before I realized that your average female is not a six-foot-tall goddess.

My mother was six-foot-one and a natural platinum blonde and I was dark and short and stocky, so obviously I must have taken after my father, whoever he may have been, which is what I say when I want to make Mim really mad. She is still stunning when she dresses up, even though she's seventy-three now and age has shrunk her a couple of inches. She makes up for it by wearing high heels. She's also pretty skinny and has lost most of her hair and has to wear a wig, but she cleans up nice, as my husband Ralph used to say. Ex-husband, I mean. If only she wouldn't smoke so much and put on airs. She acts like a female impersonator's idea of an elegant woman. Campy, you know. Sometimes I actually think she is a gay man trapped in a woman's body.

The real trouble is that her mother sent her to finishing school and she got the idea that she comes from impoverished gentility, which is sort of true since her grandparents were the Bottlesons of Philadelphia, but by the time my mother came along they were nothing but poor farmers, the family fortune having been wiped out in a depression in the 1870s or '80s, I forget just when. I hate to think what my grandmother had to sacrifice to send Mim to that damn silly school. Some people live in a world of their own, don't they? Anyway it must have been while Mim was in that school that she got knocked up. So a lot of good it did to send her there.

There have been times I've said to her, "Mim, you're a Las Vegas show girl and that's what you've been all your adult life. Parading around with the entire Eiffel Tower on your head and your tits hanging out. So why don't you stop walking around with your nose in the air." I only say that when I have to, because it hurts her feelings. But I happen to know that on her family farm all they had was an outhouse, and here she comes having a fit when she discovers I have no sewage to my trailer and have to carry my waste to Sam's outhouse twice a week in a portable toilet. "My toilet is sealed, Mim," I say, "and now we have modern chemicals so there's no odor. Now tell me your outhouse didn't stink to high heaven."

"We didn't have any choice," she says. "You have a choice."

"I choose between the lesser of many evils," I say.

"What evils?" she says, as if she didn't know.

I think it was a terrible disappointment to my mother that because of my height I had no prospects as a show girl because she thinks that's one sure way to marry a rich guy even if he may be an idiot. She should know, she married three of them. But she doesn't like to be reminded they were all idiots. She says, "Don't sniff. They put you through the best schools, you've had all the advantages. And I have a comfortable retirement, not a thing to worry about." What she means by comfortable is she owns a swanky condo on the edge of the desert and can afford to have her face lifted every two years. Well, I tell you.

And of course what she means about the best schools and all the advantages is that I should be doing something swell with my life and not be living in a nineteen-foot travel trailer in a seedy disaster of a campground in Dead Cat, Utah, population two, including me. What she means by something swell is being a writer or an architect or some other damn feminist thing and I say to her, "Mim, doesn't it occur to you that maybe I have different standards than you? Living in the Vista de Nada Condo Clone Village is not my idea of swell. I like it here. I like air I can breathe without choking. Back-to-back shopping malls and bumper-to-bumper traffic all day long is not my idea of comfortable living."

"The coyotes eat your cats," she says.

"That's one of the things you learn to live with," I say.

"Have you explained that to your cats?" she says.

"The smog in Vegas made me sick," I say.

"That's one of the things people learn to live with," she says, and she's serious.

But anyway, I got a degree in English—Mim didn't get a divorce from No. 2 until after he put me through college—and I was going to teach, but I came out into the job world in the fifties just as the communist scare was at its height and all the schools were requiring loyalty oaths. I wouldn't sign one, so I couldn't get a job. So much for something swell. Mim said at the time, "Sign it, it doesn't mean a thing." I said, "It's the principle of the thing. Didn't they teach you anything about principles in that fancy school you went to?", because by that time I was already talking to her like that, even though I was only twenty-one. I was on to her already.

So I got work as a bookkeeper trainee at the Sahara Club and that's where I met Ralph. He was a croupier at first, then later a pit boss. By the time we got married he had become a bartender. After we'd been married a while I asked him why he changed career paths and he said he could knock down more money as a bartender—it's hard to cheat if you're working the tables or supervising. Management is on to all the tricks and those boys are tough. What I didn't know till later was that at the bar Ralph was doing more than knocking down some of the drink money. He was pimping and dealing drugs and god knows what else. And then when his shift ended he'd gamble.

He always gave me his paycheck, he was conscientious about that, but he said his tips and anything he made on the side were his. It was years before I realized how much that was, and even more years before I realized he lost more at the gaming tables than he made on the side and we were up to here with the money lenders. Well, I tell you. That was that.

But the real reason the marriage failed is he was lousy in bed. When I still thought I could save the marriage I read some psychology books about gamblers and they said gamblers are usually impotent. It has to do with how they feel about themselves and why they gamble, and I'm here to tell you it's the truth. I don't know why I put up with him so many years except that he was charming and sweet, the gambler's stock in trade. How do you think they keep borrowing all that money.

Mim never did like Ralph, she saw right away he was a lost cause and never let me forget it once we got divorced. "Never marry a man named Ralph," she says. "Name me one Ralph that ever amounted to anything."

"Ralph Nader."

"He amounted to something?"

"Don't be nasty. Ralph Waldo Emerson. You can't tell anything by a name, Mim, look at us. We're both Miriams and we're not anything alike."

"That's what you think," she says, which makes me really mad.

So anyway by the time I divorced Ralph I was head

bookkeeper at another club which I won't name, and I was making pretty good money, but by then I knew a lot about keeping books and I knew some things didn't jibe. Management brought in outside accountants to do the taxes and they never found any problems but they were probably paid to make things look right.

The club declared all their gaming income, all right, it wasn't that. It was that they declared much more money than they took in. There are formulas and statistics that predict what you should be taking for X number of games on such-and-such a night and all that. I knew more money was ending up in receipts than people could possibly be losing at those tables, you know what I mean? It was clear I was smack in the middle of a huge money-washing operation. So I thought I'd better get out of there before the feds got wise and came snooping around. I was innocent of any wrong-doing but after all I was the head bookkeeper. Are they going to believe I don't know what's going on?

I knew I wouldn't go to work for another club where I might get in the same position again and I didn't know what else I was going to do to earn money. I had some savings I hadn't told Ralph about and we had sold the house and split the proceeds during the divorce so I knew I could live for a while but I thought I'd better get my living expenses down as low as possible because who knows. So I bought the travel trailer, which was the beginning of the trouble between Mim and me about the way I live. She said, "It isn't even really nineteen feet long. They measure that thing you hook to the truck to tow it. . . . "

"The tongue."

" . . . and that's four feet right there . . . "

"Three."

" . . . all right, three, but you still don't have but sixteen feet of living space, hardly bigger than my bedroom. There's not even room for my legs under your table."

"Why don't you get ordinary two-and-a-half-foot legs like everybody else, then you'd fit."

"Don't change the subject. That's no way to live."

"It is if you're unemployed, Mim."

"I'm unemployed and look at me."

"I have."

Ralph said once, "Face it, your mother was a hooker." This was when I told him I read that the big gaming clubs never opened up in Vegas until the late forties. Before that it was a gambling town all right, but before organized crime decided to build their own Oz it was small time stuff. I didn't think there was anything like the shows they have now. I doubted it. So where did my mother work?

"Three guesses," said Ralph, "and the first two don't count."

"I remember being backstage, though."

"Your mother was seventeen when she hit town. They

met her getting off the bus. Trust me, I know about these things. It was probably a burlesque house you remember. You were sleeping in one dressing room, she was tricking in another."

"That's a hell of a way to talk about my mother."

"You're the one with the doubts."

So anyway it wasn't long after I moved into the trailer when there was a knock on the door one afternoon and without thinking, I opened the door wide to see who it was. Well, I tell you, it's one thing to be sitting in a movie theater and see a Thing with a monster face rise from the swamp all covered with gore, it's quite another to open your own front door and see a real live Thing dripping blood all over your door step, with purple and red pulp where its face ought to be, standing there two feet in front of you. It didn't take me one full second to slam that door shut, but it had no sooner banged into place than I realized, My god, it's Ralph. So I opened the door again just as fast, and Ralph had his fist raised ready to pound on the door again and I yelled, "Ralph, don't!" thinking he was going to hit me.

The goons from the money lenders had left him in a ditch no more than half a mile from the trailer park, right on Tropicana Avenue across the street from the airport, with thousands of people in cars streaming by, and no one had noticed. And he walked all the way to my trailer with his face like that and nobody stopped to ask if he needed help. They probably thought he was just made up for some stunt in a show, walking along calm as you please in broad daylight. Well, I tell you. He wanted me to fix him up and I said, "Ralph, I can't make a cow out of hamburger, you need a surgeon," but he wouldn't go to Emergency because he was sure they would call the police. "That would really fix things," he said. We were both so upset we didn't even think of the obvious lie, that he got mugged, so I cleaned him up best I could and gave him a sleeping pill.

When he woke up he said "Miriam, I need to borrow your house money." I said, "No way." He said, "You're signing my death warrant." I said, "You signed that yourself when you got mixed up with those psychos." But he turned on the charm and sang his gambler's siren song and he almost had me convinced when I asked him how much he owed. Turns out my house money would pay only about half of it. I said, "They'll beat you up for the other half so what good is it gonna do to take all my money?" He said, "It'll hold things up until I have a chance to get out of the hole." Then I realized that Ralph wasn't going to use my money to pay off his debt. He was going to use it as a stake to try to win enough to pay the whole thing. He wasn't ever going to get out of the hole, not ever, and my money wasn't going to save him and then two people would be ruined instead of just one, and besides I wasn't married to him anymore. So I not only said "No," I pushed him out the door with on old cotton shirt torn up and tied around his face for a bandage.

A day or two later it occurred to me: Maybe they don't know we're divorced. Maybe they'll come after *me* for the money.

"Who do you think you're kidding," Mim said. "They know everything about him, including the divorce. They won't touch you. They'll figure they'd do him a favor to mess you up."

But I left town anyway. I went down to where Ralph lives and left him my little blue Volvo, stuck the keys and a note in his mailbox, and took his '64 Plymouth station wagon, which I still had a set of keys for. I needed something to pull the trailer and although the Plymouth was about on its last legs, it had more power than the Volvo, and it still had a hitch on it from some previous owner.

I barely made it up that long grade on I-15 to Utah, up the Virgin River Gorge and through St. George and on up and up and up to Cedar City, but that plucky old Plymouth kept going somehow until I took it in my head—I don't know what possessed me—to turn off the main highway into what is still some of the most remote country in the west.

Then the Plymouth threw a rod.

It happened right outside a campground called the Dead Cat, sitting all by itself, with no campers in it that I could see, miles from anywhere. The dirtiest man I ever saw came walking out to see what was what. He looked about a hundred years old and walked like he had a cargo hook for a spine and he had about a week's stubble on his chin and a hat that looked like he cleaned his truck's dip stick with it. He had some kind of pink lenses in his glasses that were so greasy it was a wonder he didn't need a white cane. Well, I tell you. But he was nice enough, and offered to ride me into Escalante, the nearest town, and when I said "How far is that?" he said, "Seventy-five miles." I said, "Can I buy a car there?" and he said, "No, for that you got to go to Cedar City or St. George," and I knew Cedar City was the closest and it was a hundred and twenty-five miles behind me.

I must have looked like I didn't know what to do because he said "Why don't you park your rig right here at Dead Cat? I got the cleanest air in five states and you won't have no noise except ravens fussing once in a while. Fifty dollars a month includes well water. If you fix yourself up a solar panel you'll have free electrics and then all you'll have to buy is propane for your cooking and your heat. I'll help you rig up your solar panel."

I thought: Well, I don't know where I'm going anyway and I might as well sit right here while I figure out what to do. So Sam, that's his name, got his truck and hauled my trailer in. Sam let me use his radio phone to call Mim but I wouldn't tell her where I was. She said, "You're being paranoid." I said, "Mim, you don't take this seriously because you didn't see

Ralph." We left the Plymouth right where it was and took the plates off and it sat there three weeks before the Highway Patrol came and towed it away.

Sam took me to Escalante for groceries and I never did make up my mind what to do. I just sort of settled in and here I am. I like having clean air to breath. I like Sam. He is seventy-four years old and except for the cargo hook he's lithe as a monkey and minds his own business. Never asked me where I was going or where I came from. I love the well water. I never knew how bad chlorine tasted until I drank this water without it. Mim says, "It isn't sterilized? You don't know what you may be drinking!" I say, "Chlorine is a deadly poison, Mim. Did you know that?"

So anyway I called Mim every week to tell her I was all right and she ranted and raved to know where I was but I wouldn't tell her. "I'm too close to retirement," I said. "I've paid social security all these years and I intend to draw on it before I die."

"You don't trust your own mother?" she said.

"Not with a knife at your throat, I don't."

"You're being paranoid, Junior," she said again. "You ought to see a counselor. I told you they have no interest in you."

"Your opinion does not make a fact," I said.

I'd been at Dead Cat only three months when Mim told

me Ralph had remarried. "I can't believe this," I said. "My body isn't even cold yet."

"She's got money."

"Then I guess I don't have to worry anymore."

"You never did. Now will you come home?"

"Vegas isn't home. You can come here."

"I like Vegas."

"I mean to visit, Mim."

"You lived your whole life in Vegas and it isn't home?"

"That's exactly right, Mim," I said, but in fact, until Mim fed it back to me the enormity of what I had said hadn't hit me. Now a lot of stuff came bubbling up through the crack. I always considered myself an ordinary, decent person just trying to get along in the world, but I also enjoyed, compliments of the gaming industry, not paying any state personal income tax or sales tax. I'd been bought. And now I had a flash of all those other ordinary decent people—sales clerks and waitresses and hotel maids and construction workers—in the super-market, bags of groceries on the floor at their feet, dead-faced, pouring their grocery change into the slot machines on their way out the exit. I'd been blind to them all these years—but not really, since the vision now came back to me with such brilliance. Las Vegas is Oz, all right, but because it was convenient I'd ignored, even when I quit my job at the casino, who was behind the curtain, who was pulling the levers and running the flashing colored lights and the Disney façades and the beautiful girls on parade and the lush hotels. I thought I was married to one weak and unfortunate man, but I was married to a corrupt system that didn't think twice about destroying people. I even took their money and told myself it was honest wages. And I couldn't even bear to think what Mim might have been through all those years. Since she was seventeen. My god.

"Miriam?"

"I'm sorry, Mim, I got distracted. Listen, I want you to come visit me. Get a pencil and I'll give you the directions."

"I'd rather just fly."

"There are no airports in the wilderness, Mim."

"Wilderness? Oh my god."

So Mim started driving up to see me about once a month. Sam fixed up an old camper shell that's been sitting on the back of the lot for god knows how many years, and I slept in it when Mim was here and gave her my bed in the trailer. She had to sleep with her legs bent. "There's not even any sidewalks," she complained, but after her first trip she bought a pair of flat-heeled shoes, about the only concession she's made to the way I live.

In January, when we had those below-zero temperatures, my pipes burst in three places. Sam fixed two of them but then we found that the third break was behind the heater, under the refrigerator, and beside the bathtub, and to get to it we'd have to take out a wall in the bathroom, and to do that we'd have to remove the bathtub ("That's a bathtub?" Mim said, "I thought it was a sink") and to remove the bathtub we'd have to take out another two walls. Since there's no way to run heat tape on those pipes because there's places underneath where you can't get to the pipes without taking out the whole bottom of the trailer, and since without heat tape the pipes will probably just freeze again anyway, we said to hell with it and Sam just ran a hose in through the kitchen window over the sink and put a nozzle on it, the kind you can turn off. I heat my water on the stove.

Mim said, "Lord, Miriam, you mean you don't even bathe anymore?"

"Of course I bathe, Mim. Just not the way you do."

Sam was there at the time, and he said, "A whore's bath, is what we used to call 'em. You splash some water under your arms and in your crotch and you're ready to go." Then he laughed that cackle laugh of his and Mim gave him a look that should have withered him, if he wasn't already about as withered as you can get and still be alive. Mim is a full foot taller than he.

Another jag Mim gets on is, What do I do with my time? I say, "I read books I've meant to read all my life. Sam and I are trying to grow those beans the Anasazi grew here a few hundred years ago. I take long walks in the canyons. I play cards with Sam. Maybe I'll write my memoirs."

"Memoirs!" Mim says. "What have you got to write about?"

The next time she came she was driving a monster Winnebago. "Mim, what on earth?" I said. "So I can stay civilized and cook in a microwave," she said. The same trip she brought me a TV. She thought all you have to do is plug it in and call the cable company. "There's no cable up here, Mim, for god's sake." So next trip she brought a VCR and half a dozen movies on tape. I have to admit Sam and I do enjoy watching movies of an evening. Now we belong to a classic-movie-of-the-month club and we're building a good collection. We've watched *Gone With The Wind* eight times.

But Mim never lets up. If it's not "What if you got seriously ill? What would you do?" it's "What about the snakes and cougars and tarantulas?" The answer to the first one is, "Die, I suppose." The answer to the second is, "You live in a city where the black widow spider population is so dense they have seats on the city council."

And of course she doesn't like Sam. At first she wouldn't go with me down to his cabin for our nightly Canasta game. "That filthy man," she said. "That place of his stinks. What does he do with all those stacks of old newspapers? Why doesn't he throw them out?"

"I don't know. I suppose he doesn't want to be responsible for ten thousand homeless mice."

"It's all those mouse droppings that stink. And Canasta is

a boring game. It went out of fashion thirty years ago, it's so boring."

"We liven things up by playing for a nickel a point," I said. That perked her interest and so she finally went with me. The month between her visits has shrunk to three weeks and whenever she comes she's the one who asks, as soon as the sun goes down, if it isn't time to go down to Sam's yet.

He's into her for $523.85 so far.

# ten

# WHERE DETAIL IN THE

# BACKGROUND IS PERMISSIBLE

*Shelley Hunt*

Upstairs there is half a studio, where I will learn to paint. I can't stand the exercises in the little book Landers bought me with all the tubes of acrylics; I want light, an impression, not this cold precision—two cowboys wet and dry-brushed into verisimilitude. I want birds that don't exist, the shadows of birds, a pretty half-bird to hang on my wall or send to my mother with a note that says, like a child's cry, I made this for you.

This is where Jacqueline comes in. She lies on my couch in the kitchen, in active labor. Her feet brace against the wall just so; close your eyes, you can see her.

"It helps me angle my pelvis the right way," she tells Landers, my husband, the man in silhouette, the one framed in the sliding glass doors. In his hands are two yellow tomatoes and one green tomatillo. A camera hangs around his neck. I'm leaning over the sink, picking sprigs of cilantro out of the herb garden on the window sill. Behind me, on the grill, chilies are roasting.

"Maybe this can wait," Landers says. He watches Jacqueline intently.

"You have to use the veggies now for maximum impact," Jacqueline says.

"Oh, right," he says. "How foolish of me."

"I want salsa," Jacqueline says. "Now."

"Hand them here, Landers," I say. He does, then returns to the doorway.

Jacqueline curls forward into herself and begins breathing.

"Like a cat, like a cat, like a cat," she says.

Landers counts under his breath: one and two and three and four and on and on to forty-six, which is when Jacqueline sinks back into the couch.

"Stop counting and take pictures," Jacqueline says. "I want to remember this."

"How could you not?" he says. But he lifts the camera, a Nikon N90, to his face and begins to click away.

What I would like to do is paint this, Jacqueline in her cat stretch, Landers in the doorway, maybe even me at the grill, but the brush is a stranger in my hand, my spastic hand—I am only contemplating brush strokes and color. At this point I can't make anything not too real either, no shapes that snag the eyes, colors that question things like four o'clock in the afternoon, tea time, when everything is fine, just fine. So what I would do, if my hands were not my hands, what I would do is draw a line that is Jacqueline on my kitchen couch, a pained sort of line, but also productive, triumphant, and maybe a few lines that brought up words no one else has. For motherhood. I chop tomato and bruise cilantro at the sink, urge Jacqueline on over my shoulder. What I would do is paint myself onto the couch, with Landers holding my hand, blood trickling sweetly down my leg.

Landers holds onto the door. He looks at Jacqueline with the same look men have at times like this, not birth times, necessarily, but women times, *what the hell are you doing with that body of yours* times. Even though I don't bleed, this look is on his face often enough. But he's a good man, not to worry, I tell my mother, and this is the truth, he's the face across from me, always puzzled, unsure, aware of me when I am not aware. Be careful, my mother says. Be wary.

And variations: Caution. Prudence. Just this side of morality, but what can you do? Chaos, Landers says, love, ought not to have pattern at all. But there you go. Everything, if played out long enough, will disappoint. Or maybe not.

I am Jacqueline's childless friend, I am the childless friend of friends, and I have stood in the gap before. In intercession. With nurses, and nurse mid-wives, and the tungsten light beside the cranked-up bed. I am the woman who follows you until you ask me to be there, to hold your hand, to help you squeeze life out of yourself and onto the blue paper and stainless steel under your hips.

Landers, standing in silhouette, says, "I'll be damned."

A small tide of water spills out of Jacqueline and onto my kitchen floor.

"Dumb luck," she says. "I just got up to pee."

"Well," I say. "You're committed now."

"Like I wasn't before," she says.

"The pains could get stronger now," I say. She shrugs on the way to the bathroom.

Landers says, "Go on in with her. Who knows what she might do in there."

This is what I heard at the doctor's office: that a small percentage of babies are born in the toilet, they fall out and swim for a moment while the mother screams. This is what Landers fears, among other things. I go and stand at the bathroom door.

"Don't bear down," I yell.

"I'm not an idiot," she yells back. "I read the flipping book."

"Oh, sweet lord," Landers says.

Something flips inside me, a fish, a tadpole, and I think for a moment of Landers' face, his father's face, all responsibility, his hand in mine, but I don't speak, not yet. Not until the paperbacks on my stomach jump, jump. Not until my stomach is larger than my breasts. Not until this hand, a claw, folds around a brush like this, without trying, and draws a sepia line from my navel to my pubic bone.

Landers says, "What about this on the floor? What do we do with this?"

"There's a mop in the pantry," I say. He knows this. This is Landers' house first of all, although he says it is ours now. And he means it, which is one of the reasons why I stay. Landers looks at me, sideways, askance, he would say.

"You want Jacqueline to do it? My hands are all tomatoed," I say.

He walks to the pantry and pulls out the mop.

"I'm throwing it away after," he says.

Jacqueline is in the bathroom, going through my makeup. I know what she's doing because the makeup drawer squeals when you try to open it quietly. Jacqueline never wears anything on her face except sunscreen without paba. Jacqueline is ten years younger than I am. Ten years ago I was bare-faced too. Makeup, I said, is bondage. I came to this conclusion on a camping trip with a friend. We were in the White Mountain wilderness, northern New Mexico. We were near the beaver pond, and I couldn't stop looking in the rearview mirror, and, once we were out of the car, the side mirror, checking my hair, my mascara. I wanted an escapade with a forest ranger, I wanted to look windblown but beautiful. Just this side of carefree. I was the girl who stood in front of the mirror adjusting my feathers, dusting the glitter off my shoulders with my mother's duster until there was just a casual trace of glitter, like I was born that way.

I want this child, this flutter like a throat tickle.

Jacqueline comes out of the bathroom with my mascara on.

"It's got eyes," Landers says. She flips him off.

"Maybe," she says, "maybe I'll do it right here. On the poker table."

"Why? Do you feel something?" Landers says.

"Go get the pail from the garage," I say. "No. The washtub. We'll need it to catch the blood."

"And the placenta," Jacqueline says.

He says, "Jacqueline, sit down, I can't stand this."

I drop the tomatoes and chilies into the food processor and push *chop*. Landers says, "I keep looking for *maim*." Short bursts, little chopping bursts, then I'm pouring salsa into terra cotta bowls. Jacqueline stands in the middle of the kitchen, dripping.

"I can't go anywhere without ruining something," she says. "I'll walk in the backyard for a while." She leans against the door frame and begins to breathe.

"Or maybe not," she says. "Get me the hell out of here."

At the hospital, Landers keeps saying, this is not my child, to every new nurse who comes in. Jacqueline folds and unfolds around the room, in and out of chairs, on her knees now, now on her side, breathing through her nose in a whine. I drink the Evian water I have packed in the labor bag and apply counter pressure. I rub lotion into her ankles, I keep the washcloth cool on her face. Landers click clicks at odd moments. The night drains through, and Jacqueline's vulva blossoms; the baby crowns. I stand to her left, holding up her leg. The child slides out onto the table, onto the blue sterile paper, head angled in an unnatural way, fists clenched. My neck hurts. The blood is vermillion, milky, staining. Landers collapses and rocks in the rocking chair, the Minolta hanging around his neck. The doctor hands the baby up, and Jacqueline turns to me, shaking that post-labor shake.

She says, "Hold her for me." I ease the child up to Jacqueline's breasts, holding her gently; Landers stands and clicks away.

There are moments when everything coalesces, when the three notes played vary, stray, and you are back in childhood, lying under your bed, or curled up behind the greasewood in the alley, hiding, listening to the others nearby, looking for you, there are moments like these. You know it. And there are moments you force, like a junkie, times when you can't stand not being found, these moments, this one right here, Jacqueline's eyes an inch from the baby, her murmurs choking all of us. This is why I come, because I am addicted to struggle, maybe even to blood.

In the morning I stand in front of the mirror and use my mascara, which so recently had bruised around Jacqueline's eyes when she wept, I use this same mascara hoping for something. I lean towards the mirror and stroke black on black, feathering out my upper lashes, gently tracing the bottom. I know how to create a look with dime-store goods. I know shadow and nuance. I know which way to stand to make the waist appear thin.

This is what Landers says, that if he had the choice, I would never shiver in the shower. What he means, I don't know. But there you are. It is his way of trying to reach across. For my birthday he bought me paints, acrylics, with white synthetic brushes and cotton canvases. I try to paint, try to see a painting, but it's difficult to begin when you don't have the wherewithal, the talent, maybe I should say. If this flutter inside me grows and forces itself into the air, then maybe I'll paint the ceiling of my craft room like a clouded sky, with a storm rolling in from the west. Maybe I'll read decorating magazines and spend money on swatches that are big enough to really see, to drape across window sills and chairs. Maybe tapestried pillows, or stripes. But first, the sky, and white gauze curtains in the window. The floor striped Payne's gray and Titanium white. This I can do.

What Landers does is smoke in the darkroom where no

one can see him and I won't wheeze all night because of it. The ceiling fan spinning, the exhaust fan sucking the bad air away, the silver chemicals bitter in his nostrils. Under his hands, faces appearing. This is the way to create a life that lasts.

Only Landers knows what he does with his camera. All the buttons and dials, I get lost. In our refrigerator where there should be eggs and cheese, we have film. And in the bathtub there are prints floating, the vinegar bitter smell through the house, white drip spots drying on the floor. Today Jacqueline spins in the water in various poses of pain. The more graphic shots are already clothes-pinned to the shower rod.

"I need more contrast," he says.

I look closely. In one, the baby is crowning, Jacqueline's knee, vulva and hand in sharp focus, the rest—my head—blurred. "I need more paper," Landers says.

"I'll go," I say.

The third store has the right paper and a pregnant woman. She wanders through the laser-disc movies, a humped up woman with baggy knees. The kind of woman with five children at home already, stacked up in what's left of her backyard like old cars, each one strangely a work of art. This is not the woman for me, I can see that. But still I follow along behind her. At the counter I ask, "When is the baby due?"

"I don't know," she says. "This time I didn't ask." She runs her hand over her belly. In the gesture I read desire, nurture, fear.

At home, Landers takes the paper and heads back into the bathroom.

"Sorry," his voice says from behind the door.

"I'll go upstairs," I say. The radio is back on, and I wander upstairs to where my paints are laid out on the credenza.

The thing is, I don't paint, have never held a brush in my hand with any real purpose. I read books, I plan in my head but nothing comes of it, nothing I would put on my wall, or show to anyone, including my mother. It's the smell and the thought that intrigues me. The names of the paints. Alizarin: This sounds to me like a hero in a fairy tale. This is a name.

I call Jacqueline; she has not yet named her child. On the phone she sounds as if she is speaking under water, as if every word floats reluctantly to the top and then bursts—not bursts, *hisses* into the air.

"Do you want me to come?" I ask. In the dead air that follows I imagine faint baby sounds.

"No," she says. "What was I thinking, Helen? Why didn't you stop me?"

"I'm coming down," I say.

"No," she says, the *o* trailing away into her breathing. "Let me sleep a while."

"I'll think up names," I say, but she has hung up. I decide to go there anyway, then change my mind. If I go and she is right, then what do I say? What I do is walk down two blocks to the house where the four women live and stop and pretend to look at their garden, which is magnificent with tiger lilies, but I'm hoping the pregnant one will be outside. I've seen her at the grocery store sometimes, but she's never alone. At least one of the other women tags along. She's a woman I would love to birth, but she's already covered. So I settle for these glances as I walk by. Something about the four of them warns me off, no trespassing.

I leave the women's house and walk down to the hospital and stand at the nursery window, looking in at the babies in their little plastic beds, little dark heads with blue or pink hats. A woman next to me snaps pictures through the glass.

"Which one is yours?" I ask.

"None," she says. "I'm shooting at the fingerprints on the glass, not the babies."

"Oh," I say.

"They'll be in there, too," she says, "but in the background, out of focus—to get the fingerprints I'm using a narrow depth of field."

I can't stop myself.

"What's that?" I ask.

She looks annoyed. She wears a blue hat.

"It's what's in focus," she says, which I think is rather minimalistic of her, but I nod. Landers, if asked the same question, would be down on the floor by now, making visual aids with the magazines and ashtrays. Maybe not. Maybe he wouldn't answer at all. It's the yes and no of him I love, after all, the now you see it, now you think you see it life I have living in the now-our house, lying in bed with him, feeling him move against me.

"As for me," she says, "never a real baby. You tell me where the fascination is."

I want to say something profound, something that will convert this woman, but all the answers, coming so soon after Jacqueline's flat hisses in my ear, all these things seem too narrow to be seriously considered.

"I've seen a baby born," I say. "More than one."

"Too much blood," she says, and shoots again at the chicken-wire glass.

"Just the right amount," I say. She lowers her camera, an Olympus something or other, and stares. I walk back to the elevator.

On the way back up the hill, I walk by the women's house again. This time she's there, the pregnant one, standing out front cutting lilies with green-handled scissors, shaking her hand between each cut. Today I feel bold, unafraid of the other women who might be watching from an upstairs window, I'm sated, maybe, from the night before; this woman, swollen, her hair pulled back and twisted up off her neck, she could be a friend, she could read me, she could meet me by the condoms and pregnancy tests and say, here, this one is fast, accurate, this one right here.

"Hello," I say. "Are those canna or calla lilies?"

"They come back every year," she says. "Is it perennials or annuals that do that?"

"I can never remember," I say. "I think perennials."

"But I think these are only day lilies," she says, "because aren't those others much bigger—the kind Georgia O'Keeffe painted?"

"I don't remember," I say, and she is bending and cutting again as I say this, angling the scissors in an unnatural way.

"Would you like me to do that?" I say.

"Oh, please," she says.

I reach through the gate and undo the latch. She holds out her hand and shows me where the scissor handles have gouged around her thumb and forefinger.

"Everything swells," she says. "My liver, my hands, my face. I'm supposed to be in bed. Could you cut this one and that one for me?"

I do so.

She says, "I'm not a bird. But I keep changing things, cutting flowers, washing the sheets until my face blows up and the headache starts and I have to lie down. I can't stop."

She sits down on the porch steps. Leaning forward the way she is, legs apart, her belly hidden by her knees and baggy green shirt, she looks a little fat, not pregnant.

She says, "I can't sit still for long." She eases back onto her elbows, then lies back against the other steps, closes her eyes.

"I'm Helen," I say, but she gestures at her stomach.

"Yes," she says. "Yes. Anytime at all now."

"That's good," I say.

I'm suddenly afraid the others are watching from the house. I pile the lilies across her belly; her fingers twitch.

"Will you be all right?" I ask. She nods, more a flinch, and I ease away and pull the gate closed behind me. I walk backwards up the block watching the lilies shudder as she breathes or the baby kicks until I can't see her anymore through the small breaks in the lilies and fence, and then I pivot, model-like, and head home, where Landers sits on the front porch waiting for me.

"Jacqueline called," he says. "She says come at seven. You can take her down some prints when you go. They're almost dry."

"What is depth of field?" I ask.

"Come here," he says, and leads me up to our bedroom. Between the windows and the kilim and my arms and breasts and his legs he explains it to me, although he knows I already know, and I know he knows, and what this is is an excuse to talk about light and things in the background that do and do not matter, and what to do in both cases.

"Go see Jacqueline," he says afterwards. I climb out of bed and look around for my underwear. Again I feel it, jump jump flutter, when I bend over.

"I'm taking the car this time," I say. He rolls onto his back and stretches.

This is how it plays out in my mind.

Jacqueline is gone, but she has left the baby for me. Not dead, just gone. She climbed out of bed and dressed and walked down the hall and to the elevator and down to the lobby where she called a cab and disappeared. On her bed she left a note explaining that I am her sister and to give me the baby who has no name. The nurses wring their hands and show me how to hold and bathe this baby. And I take this baby away with me in a rented carseat and I name her JoanCatherineAnnaMaireLindseyNaomeIoneKaelaBette but first I show her to the camera lady who is now hanging around the hospice doors looking to photograph something insignificant with death in the background. And Jacqueline moves into the women's house with lilies, and lays her hands on another's swollen belly, and watches me walk up and down the alley with her child hanging around my neck in a sling.

But what happens is this: Jacqueline lies in her bed looking like a queen, beckons me in with her hand, motions gracefully to the plastic bed where her child, Rose Elaine, sleeps. She has me call the nurse and demand a new ice pack. She says, bring me salsa. She leafs through the photographs, looking at them sometimes sideways, out of the corner of her eye, lips pursing.

I still like this ending, even though I play a smaller role, even though there is much less crying and hand-wringing and car seats and I don't convert the camera woman. I don't need to. Let her paint *trompe l'oeil* babies in her dining room and call them *putti*. Let her pretend. Or maybe not pretend, maybe be happy without this craving for blood and connection to all those other women who have gone before me. Jump, jump, swish like a basketball player beneath my hand, this fear that isn't real at all, not yet. Not until my blood splashes on the stainless steel and Landers's hands.

I take Jacqueline's hand and place it above my pubic bone.

"There," I say.

"Don't do it," she says. "Stop right now." But when Rose murmurs in her plastic bed, she says, take care, be careful, be full of care.

# eleven

# SISTERWIVES:

# THE ORDER THINGS TOOK

*Lynne Butler Oaks*

He can see me from where he is standing, off down the row along with his dogs. I know, because I can see him too. And from where I am, I'm seeing and thinking how he is keeping his eyes on us new kids. We're in from Garden City and Laketown with some, like me, even thumbing it up the canyon from Logan to earn our next-year's school clothes, us all lying about our ages and saying we've picked berries before. I am the first to get caught in my lie. He sees me resting my flat on one arm, dropping berries into it from my other hand, and he comes up the row hot-neck hollering.

"You're breaking the berries into bits doing it like that," Reuben Powers shouts. "You want nothing but bruises?"

I let the flat fall.

He moves in, a big man standing so close I can smell the soil on his skin. He says, "It's like slipping off a shoe."

At that, Reuben unbuckles the leather belt I have around my waist. He slips it out of the pant loops. He hangs it around my neck so the buckle and stitched ends lay down in front like a field snake—its tail and its head. These ends Reuben hooks onto one of the wire-handled Crisco cans that litter the ground. He makes with it a makeshift bucket that falls down to where I am just becoming breasted. So now I'm holding nothing. I watch while Reuben lifts my two hands up. He wraps one set of my fingers around the thorny stem of the bush, holds them there tight till I get stinging little cuts. He takes my other hand then, the fingers of it, and places them, very lightly, around the berry. And then it is us, together, sliding the berry off its bulb.

"It's like slipping off a shoe," Reuben Powers says again. "Both hands," he says, "always both hands."

I now hold mine up to his face. I fly my fingers about like a Flamenco dancer, showing him they are free, me saying how really sorry I am over and over and laughing. Reuben Powers, not even watching me anymore, picks up my flat and drops it halfway up the row so I'll be moving toward it.

"Never laugh around adults or men," the girl across from me says. "Big, big mistake," she says. Then she reaches through the bush and tweaks my nipple where it shows through the cloth of my cotton t-shirt and goes back to her own picking. The girl's name is Libby.

Libby is again here with me now. Some time has passed. We're underground, in Reuben's raspberry cellar, on the far side of his fields.

"Get that blanket up on your head," Libby says to me. "It keeps the blood hot in your skull," she is saying. I've just been baptized. I'm now dripping a puddle onto the roughed up cement floor. It is cool here and I hop back and forth, making small splashes, warming my toes. Libby unbuttons the buttoned front of my soaked-through shirt. It is white, this shirt, and one of Reuben's. A white shirt like the white shirts he wears every day.

Here's the way it went for my baptism. "Having been commissioned of Jesus Christ," Reuben said, "And in the name of the Father and of the Son and of the Holy Ghost I baptize you, Evie Powers." And Reuben, his arm under my back, plunged me under then, laying me down backwards, my knees bending, him pushing my body down all the way into the Bear Lake water, me holding my stomach in tight so it did not pop up, did not break the water line, null-and-voiding it all.

But my baptism isn't all there is today. Now Libby and me twirl and dance undone the wound-tight blanket from my head. Libby helps me slip the very nearly satin dress over my dripping hair. My dress is all eggshell cream except for ribbons falling down like fringe from the sleeves. I've ribbons of every color—yellow, blue, and even deep pink—these ribbons being Libby's idea, her saying pure white makes us women look too dangerous for words. Libby ties colored ribbons also in my hair. I am shivering and almost ready.

Except for Libby I am parted from my past here. And you will understand this, how that with me being just fifteen what I am thinking about now is my mother—my mother who stayed in town, her pleading "no, no, no," and please don't call for my father to come. Her also saying that, in this religion of Reuben's, Husbands-Fathers-God is like a Trinity, one and complete, so there is no point to taking or giving away, just the time of life you are in and who you belong to in it.

Libby says to me, "Don't worry." Do not worry. Libby says mothers all have something to hide, and that no is always a lie anyway, an escape hatch, a word to fall back on. Libby is a comfort to me, her knowing things and talking like she does in circles that come back around. Libby knows things.

Libby knows about mothers because her own mother has mothered seven. And she knows about Mormons because she stayed one up until last year when she turned thirteen. My mother is a Mormon, also, but she's one of the up-to-date Mormons nobody's really scared of. What scares my mother is what the up-to-date Mormons call Reuben Powers, and will now call me too, which is a *Fundamentalist,* a splinter.

Reuben wears white for the wedding too. Even his shoes. Reuben wears what he has baptized me in, him just letting it all sun dry for the covenants, adding only a green colored tie, the leaf of Adam. Now we two are standing together, Reuben and me in front, my two sisterwives, these being Reuben's first wives, are back behind. And we vow our vows, solemn and sacred, on Reuben's back porch and in view of his fields.

"God, god, god," Libby says when I'm married. "You look just fine. Almost absolutely safe." She says, "Nothing showing."

Libby strips a ribbon from my hair. God is the last word most Mormons will ever say. She says, "I'll visit." Libby knows I am even now carrying a baby. Libby is the one I told.

After the wedding I wait for Reuben. I'm thinking he will lead me into our new bedroom. I am thinking he'll lead me there to do what we did first in that same dug-out cellar where I was earlier changing. That cellar with its heavy metal door lifting up like a lid from the ground, its cement steps going down. I picture him coming in now and saying something like, "This, Evie, this is not for God" (so much of this day having been for God). I picture him saying, "This, Evie, is for love."

And then I'm waiting and thinking how silent and sad Reuben was all through that first love. That love being our only love together, my first love at all—it being painless—just smooth stretching muscles and damp. That love being simple, after all, being as easy, really, as Reuben laying me out over a pile of stiff wool blankets, the hairy linseed scent of them mixing with the innocent wet-sand smell of water seeping in from the walls, water coming up through the floor. And it was Reuben rubbing my breasts and my face, with his hands soft and rough, like dirt-covered berries on your tongue, him pushing inside me, saying nothing at all, me saying nothing either, only breathing, and me watching his face block then unblock the sight of the bare light bulb up over our heads.

So now Libby is on her way down the canyon and I am up here watching the door for Reuben to come through it and be close with me again. While I wait I light candles from the Antique and Rock Shop—apricot scented, and plum. I put some near the old green army bed that takes up most of the bedroom. I move one of the lit candles to the kitchen table. I sit with a cup of hot lemon water, the lemon tasting like the smell of Bear Lake in the morning.

The door opens and it isn't Reuben. It is Willa, the oldest of my sisterwives. Willa is carrying a plastic bag of underdeveloped cucumbers.

"Where's Reuben?" I say.

Willa takes my elbow, says, "Evie, I want you to know we're all pleased. But, well, circumstances."

"Where's Reuben?" I say.

"Reuben's covenant with God . . . is . . . you understand."
Willa starts up again, speaking slowly and handing me the
cucumbers. "Well, it means that he can have relations only to
replenish the earth." She keeps speaking but I stop hearing.

I say, "Where's Reuben?"

Willa says, "Do you understand? Exactly, then? What I
mean?" I say, "Where's Reuben?"

"I mean sexual," she says. Willa talks on. Reuben, I find
out from her, will spend three nights in the small house which
is because, Willa says, it is simply not necessary that everyone
know that there was already one coming. Reuben having
repented, she said, there was no need at all for them to start
wagging their tongues.

After the three days she, Willa, will move back to the main
house with him, Willa says. For now though, she will stay with
us, Reuben having asked her to. Reuben saying, or so Willa
says, that my voice is trouble for him, a temptation, it being
low and raspy from a bad tonsillectomy.

When Reuben comes into the house, I run to him and hold
him so my belly with Baby in it is pressed against his belt
buckle. My arms I wrap tight. Reuben has his dogs along, Blue
Tic hounds he calls Sundance and Kid. Sundance is still on the
porch, pushing in at the screen, yelping. Reuben pulls me in
close and hugs me back. "Go ahead and let Sundance in," Willa
says, and I am not surprised. Everyone had been told by
Reuben about Willa keeping Sundance always at her side due

to what it was that happened with her own baby. It's the first story I heard about Willa, and Reuben always lets her tell it herself for its message. It is one of those stories you carry around and can't put down.

The story about Willa's own baby is this: that one day when she was out picking berries, being maybe three months carrying, she began to feel pains. At first she thought she just maybe had to water so she went behind a tree and lifted her skirt. But as she slid her underpants down to her knees, a pulpy clot fell out of her onto the ground. Willa struggled to get out of her underpants, she said. She wanted to use them, you see, to wrap around her baby, which was just this clot but, still, her baby. But before Willa could get her feet loose—and here is the part with the message—before Willa could get her feet loose from her underpants, Sundance bounded up and ate what it was that was lying there in the field at Willa's feet.

The story goes that Willa did not scream. Did not cry. Willa just started singing about grace and she sang all day long. Sundance began having seizures after that, though. Seizures that cause his eyes to fix and roll upwards and his nose to foam, giving the dog spasms that even to this day send stuff spewing out of his mouth.

"Come on in Sun," Reuben says, opening the door.

Sundance bounds straight for Willa. Willa scratches behind his ears and hugs his neck, touching the collar she's leather-burned for him. The collar that says "God's Light."

Later, Reuben sits us down across the table where we are eating potato pancakes fixed by Willa. He says to me, "When I am not here you should make the house appear absolutely empty. No lights after dusk," he says. "Curtains drawn."

"Are we hiding?" I say.

"We don't want to draw attention," Reuben says. "We have broken the law. Man's."

I don't want to hide. It is something Libby, and probably even my mother, would refuse to do. But mostly I don't want Reuben on the floor with my heart while Willa's too-strong-and-solid body is lying in the bed next to me and my raspy voice, which is what I almost say. But before I do speak up, Reuben pats my head, kisses me on the cheek and kneels with us. We kneel down, then, and hear Reuben pray a prayer to God for sanctification—his, mine, and Willa's—Reuben holding our hands, Sundance circling around.

I see Willa often, and most times she comes with Dawn, my second sister wife. As is usual for them, they come for these visits carrying jam or dried fruit or books in chapter and verse. As is also usual, it is from these books that I learn about the wine cup of God's fury, about His wars and rumors, about His love.

"There will come a day when none of us can hide even the smallest act," Dawn says as often as she says anything. Dawn saying that in heaven our private times and flaws will be shown big-screen to precisely those people we most don't want to see them.

Dawn likes me less than Willa. Dawn never raises her voice. Libby would say Dawn is one of those people who feels most powerful when she gets friends to betray each other out of kindness.

Libby would say: "Watch your back." But here's what I would say to Libby. I would say that I am not afraid of anyone who really and truly includes me in, and I could prove it too, and would. I would and could make her understand the weight and comfort of belonging.

Willa, Dawn, and all of us meet almost daily in the big house. It is we three and also many other wives and children belonging to the Church of the Lamb. Reuben has eight children, this being a great pride, many quivering arrows. We first hold the devotional, the singing and scriptures. Today Dawn teaches the lessons. The young sons draw pictures of Abraham and the ram that was just for show and also Isaac, Abraham's real sacrifice to his father, this drama proving all about obedience being the first and largest of all possible laws. Could you give up your own child for God? the boys are asked.

For our young girls, Dawn asks me to pass around a fresh orchid or rose, telling them to handle it, to press and rub the petals with their fingers, showing how things get spotted and bruised if they let themselves get touched too early and in the wrong way. It goes of course without saying, no one says it, that I myself am the living example of this, the unspoken object lesson for the other girls, the very truth of it all, capital T.

Our lessons all learned, we start our worthy work. The oldest woman here, Jenna, makes loaves of dough that we freeze. Willa woodburns names into the caskets of God's true saints, children who die before they turn eight, too worthy for this world. Me, I hand letter labels for the jam we'll sell in gift shops and raspberry shake stands around town. I drop one jar for every ten I put labels on though. I drop the jars, regular as a tithe, and listen to them break, break, breaking. I see for myself how the jam spills out, turns to oxblood, makes dark ribbon streaks on the hardwood floor. Willa and Dawn often catch me at my game. When they frown over my direction I shrug my shoulders and smile back—like what I'm saying is that being pregnant makes you a clutz, so there, it does. I smile, eyes up, until I've made them smile back, which I know they always will.

Reuben makes our extra money fighting fires in the nearby hills. On days like today, when Reuben visits me, he comes in through the back door smelling of smoke, an old smell, like spent bullet casings. Even on these days he's wearing a clean, white shirt and he carries in his breast pocket a vial of consecrated oil. We talk a little. He holds my hand.

Today the oil is for me. This oil he puts in my hair, laying on his hands and blessing my body, in the name of the Father and of the Son and of the Holy Ghost, that it might deliver a healthy servant of God, valiant seed, Amen. Reuben lifts his hands from the crown of my head and leaves for the main house. I'm alone and I start up with touching the oily place there in my hair. It feels slick and sticky and warm and it's making my mind flash back to that clot, it's making me think and see, too, that bloody clot falling out of Willa, it's causing me to picture that clot now being bloody up there on my head. And then when I'm touching it I can't help myself. I can't help myself from yelping high and sharp and on and on until soon I'm suddenly howling like a dog, which no one, praise Jesus, hears me do.

The hills where Reuben fights fires are the same hills where Reuben's brother died in the worthiest of all possible ways. At first we'd wanted to believe he had died in the fire, the fire he and Reuben were fighting. But then it came out when they studied him that Reuben's brother perished a martyr after all, cut under the throat from ear to ear by some false prophet. Reuben, after this, became our newest prophet and revelator. It was his calling, everyone agreed. Reuben now says to his congregation that it was through his older brother that he learned about love. Reuben tells how his mother once tied the boys' suspenders together, once strung them up over the clothesline out back. How there she pulled old socks up over their fists, and made them box, arms flying, legs dangling. She'd made them box until they had tears, then she'd lowered them down and hugged them to each other so they could say "Love you" and "Love you, too."

This true parable from his life has insights without number, Reuben says. For instance, that violent things should never be done with meanness, and did we understand the distinction?

Reuben grows a beard to look like his brother. Reuben marries his brother's wives, Shen and Claire and Vicki Powers, to take care of them. Being our leader meant Reuben had other tests, too. Fasting twenty-four hours, then forty-eight, then 96. Laying on hands. Prophecies. Weeping.

Some weekends Libby still comes up the canyon to see me. "Don't knock," I say. "It's supposed to be empty." So Libby walks right in. Today she finds me naked on the bed, me with my enormous stomach. "God, god, god," Libby says at the sight.

Libby later says, "So when can you finally be with him again," her slurring out the word *be* like it's dirty. And what does he do at night up in those hills she wants to know.

I say he loves me, he does, and Libby shakes her head like I've spent my whole penny.

"It's impossible to want what you already have," Libby says. "Especially for men but for women, too." Libby traces the stretch marks that are beginning to ribbon my stomach pale pink and white.

"We're just waiting until after," I say. And after, I tell her, I'll cover these marks up with the strawberry silk slip I've saved from my mother.

"Grow up," Libby says. She says, "Buy peppermint mouthwash and learn to swallow it, touch a little of it down there on your name-it-not."

Libby leaves and after I think about time with Reuben, time after Baby. I'll take a long bath in this unlit house, I'm thinking, a bath with bubbles from vanilla shampoo. I'll rinse my hair in eggs.

It's late spring, the day I move to the main house for my birthing. There is frost. For my sake, Willa makes Sundance stay out in the yard. When the pains begin seizing me, I move to a room where I am surrounded by women I know from devotional.

There is haze sometimes. There is even, eventually, me singing children's songs, "Row, Row, Row" and "Old McDonald," and me begging the women to come up with strange and difficult animals so my mind will have to leave the pain to find the right voice. There's pain going out and pain returning. Pain and then the absence of pain and always there's water, or something like water, seeping away. Through it, the women talk quietly, birds through a closed window. Outside in the yard the dogs, or black shadows of them, move in and out of the trees.

When he is born, Baby stays silent. Slapping him makes him start, but not cry. And Willa, the one who has pulled him out, gets carried away. Finally, I say for the slapping to stop. Willa hands Baby to Dawn, who nurses him, him going on and living after all, me falling asleep.

Six weeks pass by and Baby still sleeps most of the time. I move back to the house at the edge of the field to rest with him. Libby hitchhikes up to see Baby and to hold him and say "God, god god."

"Truckers," she says as she lowers Baby back onto the bed. "They keep asking you to get them the map off the dash so they can see your you-know-whats when you lean forward."

I don't laugh and Libby acts up like she's getting angry. "What's wrong?" she says. "Is it something?" She says, "Tell me, tell me, tell me, Evie, just what the hell is the matter with you?"

The matter is that Baby, even asleep, surrounds me. That is, at least, what I'm supposing the matter is. I watch Baby's chest rise and fall. I take him often into the cooling cellar. I keep it dark, so his breath will show, like smoke. Then I drum other noises out of my ears and listen for strangled throat sounds. "Don't forget about the dog," is what I say to myself.

I look at Baby and say, "Watch for foam at his nose."

I've told Libby her visits are making me tired and she has stopped coming, which is just as well, now that I have Baby, who I am aware cannot know what Libby's profanity means (I'm not crazy) but whose brain might be storing up its own little record of the time after time after time that Libby takes the Lord's name in vain.

Also, I stop going to devotional. Instead, I draw the borders on the jam labels in the cooling cellar until my fingers turn blue. Even alone, I let some jars drop to the floor, smiling just to myself. No one says for me to stop.

No one begs for me to come back to devotional either. But after barely two months it's raspberry season again and Reuben needs his cellar for newly picked berries.

"How's my lamb?" he says when he comes down to visit. He says, "You need to stop spending so much time down here." He says snakes. Today Reuben reaches up and twists the overhead bulb tighter into its socket, making it bright.

"I think I could do it again," I say. "I think I could conceive." I stand up from the wool blankets and stretch my torso so that the pink lace of my slip slips out above my skirt to rest on the bare skin of my hipbone.

Reuben kisses the top of my head, then he kisses the top of Baby's head.

I get Reuben's meaning. Reuben Powers means no more babies for now and for me to stop living in the cellar.

I move out of spending my days underground, but still I refuse to pick berries. The most I can do, I tell my sisterwives, is to watch their children along with Baby while they work the fields. When I say this Willa and Dawn look at each other like they are a couple, like a mother and father even, and I am the child. Reuben later stands up for me, though, and they go along. He says for them to bring their children to me the night before picking, what with them having to be in the fields by dawn.

"A fire's started up in the hills," Willa says when she brings her five. "All that fasting come to naught."

I get out of bed, where I have stayed buried today, half-awake, listening to the new pickers and all their languages checking in. I go out onto the porch to look at the fire with Willa. It has started like they always do, at the edges. Soon it will send sparks flying inside, starting new little blazes that will grow, making fires as pretty as sunsets. As pretty as paintings of sunsets. What this hillfire means is that Reuben will go, that the women will have to bring the berries in alone.

Willa and Dawn pretend not to notice the state of my house, my slept-in shirt. They warm milk for the children and put cinnamon in it. They go back to their own houses to sleep until morning. The milk stays on the counter getting cold.

When it gets late, the children lie down. Soon the sound of them gets softer, then silent. I go back to bed, too, but I don't sleep. Around midnight I take Baby from the dresser drawer full of pillows. I take Baby down into the cooling cellar and lay him on the wool blankets. The light is so weak I can barely see, and it is cold, too, which makes Baby cry, the sound of him reaching my ears like underwater.

"We need our own fire," I say to Baby. "Fire to get warm is just what we need." I tear one blanket into strips. I pick up the kerosene lamp, light it for its flame. "Wait for me," I say.

I circle Reuben's fields with the lighted strips of wool. I dance them around, Maypole ribbons on the first day of May. I dance and the fire begins to make its music. A soft hiss in the distance. The echo of drums coming.

Only when the sound of the fire I have started is too loud to bear do I start back down into the cellar. I hold the heavy lid up, stand on the top of the cellar steps, watching and listening for as long as I can. I can see everything from here. The hill fire, far off, making its pictures, and now the field fire, too. Reuben's fields growing bright with light, rows of light leaning toward the hills, toward the houses. Light surely warming mine and all the sleeping children.

When the acid smell of the smoke makes it hard to breathe, I lower the tin lid. I hold Baby in my arms, in the dark, and soon we can hear Sundance, his wild barks ricocheting from above the ground, first near, then farther off, then directly overhead. Mixed with the sound of his barking and the roar of the fire is the smaller sound of drumming, rain-like drumming on the lid of the cellar. Beating fists? Running feet? Children's voices? Or maybe just the crying sound of eager birds.

"We mustn't worry," is what I say to Baby. "We just must not worry." What burns is purified and becomes the purest of all things, I am saying. What burns is bathed in gold, and after, when what is burned is only smoke, it is the whitest smoke. It is the whitest smoke, I am saying to Baby. It is the purest white. All of it drifting and curling and rising like beautiful writing toward the highest circle of heaven.

# twelve

# WALTZING THE CAT

*Pam Houston*

For as long as Julie can remember, her parents have eaten vicariously through the cat. Roast chicken, amaretto cheese spread, rum raisin ice cream—there is no end to the delicacies her parents bestow on Suzette. And Suzette, as a result, has developed, in her declining years, a shape that is at first glance a little horrifying. It isn't simply that she is big—and she is big, weighing in at twenty-nine pounds on the veterinarian's scale—but that she is alarmingly out of proportion, her tiny head, skinny tail and dainty feet jutting out from her grossly inflated torso like a circus clown's balloon creation, a nightmarish cartoon cat.

Julie remembers picking Suzette out of a litter of squealing Pennsylvania barn cats, each one no bigger than the palm of her hand. Julie was sixteen years old then, and she zipped

Suzette up inside her ski jacket and drove back to the city with her brand-new license in the only car she has ever really loved, her mother's blue Mustang convertible—the old kind—passed on to Julie and then sold, without her permission, when she went away to college.

Suzette was tiny and adorable, mostly white with black-and-brown spots more suited to a dog than to a cat, and a muddy-colored smudge on her cheek that Julie's mother would always call her coffee stain. But too many years of bacon grease and heavy cream have spread her spots huge and mis-shapen across her immense and awkward body, her stomach hanging so low to the ground now that she cannot walk but only waddle, throwing one hip at a time out and around her stomach, and dragging most of her weight forward by planting one of two rickety front paws.

Suzette has happily accepted her role as family repository for all fattening foods. She is, after all, a city cat who never did much playing or exploring anyway, even when she was thin. She didn't really chase her tail even when she could have caught it, and the places she used to like to get to under her own power: the side board of the dining room table or the middle of the king-sized bed, Julie's parents are happy, now, to lift her. Suzette has already disproved all the veterinarian's threats about eating herself to death, about Julie's parents killing her with kindness. This year as Julie turns thirty, Suzette will turn fifteen.

The cat and Julie were always friends until Julie left home and fell in love with men who were raised in and smelled like foreign places. Now when Julie comes home for a visit the cat eyes her a little suspiciously, protective, Julie thinks, like an only child.

Julie doesn't have any true memories of her parents touching each other. She has seen pictures of the year before she was born when they look happy enough, look like two people who could actually have sex, but in her lifetime, she's never seen them hug.

"Everything was perfect with your father and me before you were born," her mother has told her, confusion in her voice, but not blame. "I guess he was jealous, or something," she says, "and then all the best parts of him just went away. But it has all been worth it," she adds, her voice turning gay, as she makes the cat a plate of sour cream herring, chopped up fine, "because of you."

When Julie was growing up, there was never anything like rum raisin ice cream or amaretto cheese spread in the refrigerator. Julie's mother has always eaten next to nothing, a small salad sprinkled with lemon juice, or a few wheat thins with her martini at the end of the day, (one of Julie's worst childhood nightmares was of her mother starving to death, one bony hand extended like the Ethiopian children on late night TV) and Julie's father ate big lunches at work and made do with what little there was at home. When Julie came home from school in the afternoon she was offered carrots and celery, cauliflower and radishes, and sometimes an orange as a special treat.

Julie has forgotten most things about her childhood, but she does remember how terrified her parents were that she would become overweight. She remembers long tearful conversations with her mother about what Julie's friends and teachers would say, what everyone in the world would say, behind Julie's back if she got fat. She remembers her father slapping her hand at a dinner table full of company (one of the times when they pretended to eat like normal people) when she, caught up by the conversation, forgot the rules and reached for a warm roll from the bread basket. She remembers that her mother bought all the family's clothes slightly on the small side so that they were always squeezing and tucking and holding their breaths, her mother saying it would remind them to eat less, feeling the constant pressure of their clothes.

What Julie knows now that she is an adult is that she was never fat, that none of them were ever fat, and she has assembled years of photographs to prove it. The first thing Julie did when she went away to college was gain fifteen pounds that she has never been able to lose.

After college, when Julie left home for good, her father, in a gesture so unlike him her mother relegated it to the beginnings of senility, began to listen with great regularity to the waltzes of Johann Strauss, and her mother, for reasons which are for Julie at the same time unclear and all too obvious, started over-feeding the cat.

In her real life, Julie lives in the mountains two thousand miles west of her parents with her husband, a man named Matthew, who is handsome and successful and who tells Julie, whenever she needs to hear it, that he would not love her even one little bit more if she managed to lose the fifteen pounds she gained in college.

Julie and Matthew have three big dogs whom they love desperately and spoil like children, although Julie discourages Matthew from giving them table scraps which she has read can lead to stomach infections. Julie and Matthew talked about having real children when they first got married, and though they both seemed to like the idea, Julie did not stop taking birth control pills, and Matthew finally stopped bringing it up.

Julie works part time in the art gallery, and part time at the homeless shelter in the city nearby, stirring huge pots of muddy-colored stew and heaping the plates with it, warm and steaming. Her free time she spends in her garden where she grows every vegetable imaginable, even the ones they say won't grow in the arid Rockies. She loves watching the tiny sprouts emerge, loves watching them develop. She even loves weeding, pulling the encroaching vines and stubborn roots up and away from the strengthening plants, giving them extra water and air. She loves cooking for Matthew whole dinners of fresh vegetables, loves the frenzy of the harvest in August and September when everything, it seems, must be eaten at once. She loves taking the extra food to the shelter, and at least for a few months, putting the gloomy canned vegetables away.

What Julie loves most of all is lying in bed on Sunday mornings with Matthew and the dogs piled on top. She feels then like she is part of everything, the moon sliding behind the mountain, the sun, up and already turning the tomatoes from green to red, the breath of the dogs and Matthew's hand on her forehead, unconditional, strong. Her life seems perfect to her then, and although she knows even as she thinks it that it isn't true, she thinks sometimes that she could lie there, perfectly content, forever.

Aside from the weight issue, which always gets them in trouble, Julie and her mother are very close. Julie told her mother the first time she smoked a cigarette, the first time she got drunk, the first time she got stoned, and at age sixteen when Julie lost her virginity to Ronny Kupeleski in the Howard Johnson's across the border in Phillipsburg, New Jersey, she told her mother in advance.

"It's just as well," her mother said, in what Julie regards now as one of her finest moments in parenting. "You don't really love him, but you think you do, and you may as well get it over with someone who falls into that category."

It wasn't the last time Julie followed her mother's advice,

and like most times, her mother turned out to be right on all counts about Ronny Kupeleski. And whatever Julie doesn't understand about her mother gets filed away behind the one thing she does understand: Julie's mother has given up everything for Julie; she will always be her harshest critic, she will always be her biggest fan.

Julie's father has had at least three major disappointments in his life that Julie knows of. The first is that he didn't become a basketball star at Princeton because his mother was dying and he had to quit the team. The second is that he never made a million dollars, or since he made a million dollars if you add the several years together, Julie guesses that he means he never made a million dollars all at one time. And the third is Julie herself, who he wanted to be blonde, lithe, graceful, and a world class tennis champion. Like Chris Evert, only thinner.

Because Julie is none of these things and will never be a world class sportsman, she has become instead a world class sports fan, memorizing batting averages and box scores, penalties and procedures, and waiting for opportunities to make her father proud. Fourteen years after Julie left home it is still the only thing she and her father have to talk about. They say, "Did you see that overtime between the Flyers and the Black-hawks?" or "How 'bout them Broncos to take the AFC this year," while Julie's mother, anticipating the oncoming silence, hurries to pick up the phone.

Julie knows that her mother believes that it has been her

primary role in life to protect Julie and her father from each other: Julie's rock music, failed romances, and teenage abortion; her father's cigarette smoke, addictive tendencies toward gambling, and occasional meaningless affairs. Julie's mother has made herself a human air bag, a buffer zone so pliant and potent and comprehensive that neither Julie nor her father ever dare, or care, to cross it.

The older she gets, the more Julie realizes that her father is basically a good person who conceives of himself as someone who, somewhere along the line, got taken in by a real bad deal. She is not completely unlike him, his selfishness, and his inability to say anything nice, and she knows that if it were ever just the two of them they might be surprised at how much they had to say to each other, if they didn't do irreparable damage. Still, it is too hard for her to imagine, after so many years of sports and silence, and he is ten years older than her mother. He will, in all likelihood, die first.

Julie's parents, she had noticed in her last several visits, have completely run out of things to say to each other. They have, apparently, irritated and disappointed each other beyond the point where it is worth fighting about. If it weren't for the cat, she realizes, they might not talk at all.

Sometimes they talk about the cat, more often they talk to the cat, and most often they talk for the cat, responding to their gestures of culinary generosity with words of praise that they think the cat, if it could speak, would say.

On a typical afternoon at her parents' house, Julie's mother might, for example, stop everything she is doing to fry the cat an egg. She'll cook up some bacon, crumble the bacon into the egg, stir it up Southwestern style, and then start cooing to Suzette to come and eat it.

The cat, of course, is smarter than this and knows that if she ignores Julie's mother's call, Julie's mother will bring the egg to her on the couch, adding maybe a spot of heavy cream to make it more appetizing.

At this point Julie's father will say, in a voice completely unlike his own, "She's already had the milky-wilk from my cereal and a little of the chicky-chick we brought her from the restaurant."

"That was hours ago," Julie's mother will say, although it hasn't quite been an hour, and she will rush to the cat and wedge the china plate between the cat's cheek and the sofa, and then everyone will hold their breath while Suzette raises her head just high enough to tongue the bacon chips out of the egg.

"We like the bak-ey wak-ey, don't we, hon," Julie's father will say.

"Yes, yes, the bak-ey wak-ey is our fav-ey fav-ey," Julie's mother will say.

Julie will watch them, and try to search her conscious and

unconscious memory for any time in her life when they spoke to her this way.

The closer Julie gets to thirty, the better she and her mother get along. It is partly an act of compromise on both their parts, Julie doesn't get angry every time her mother buys her a pleated Ann Taylor suit, and Julie's mother doesn't get angry if Julie doesn't wear it. They had one bad fight two years ago on Christmas eve, when Julie's mother got up in the middle of the night, snuck into Julie's room, took a few tucks around the waist of a full, hand-painted cotton skirt Julie loved, and then washed it in warm water so that it shrunk further.

"Why can't you just accept me the way I am?" Julie wailed, before she remembered that she was in the house where people didn't have negative emotions.

"It's only because I adore you baby," her mother said, and Julie knew, not only that it was true, but also that she adored her mother back, that they were both people who needed to be adored, and the fact that they adored each other was one of life's tiny miracles; they were saving two other people an awful lot of work.

When she is at her home in the mountains Julie doesn't speak to her parents very much. She lives a life that they can't conceive of, a life that breaks every rule they believe about the world getting even. She knows that she has escaped from what her parents call reality by the narrowest of margins, and that if she ever tries to pull the two worlds together the impact will break her like a colored piñata, all her hope and humor spilling out.

One summer night, when she and Matthew have stayed in the garden long after dark planting tomatoes by the light of a three-quarter moon Julie feels a tiny explosion in the core of her body, not pain exactly, nor exactly joy, but a sudden melancholic relief, the snap of the last line that's been holding a boat too tightly to shore.

"Something's happened," she says to Matthew, though that is all she can tell him, and Matthew wipes the dirt off his hands and wraps them around her and they sit for a long time in the turned-up dirt before he takes her inside and to bed.

When the phone rings the next morning, so early that Matthew doesn't pick it up until just after the machine does, and Julie hears her father say her name once, something she has never heard before in her voice, something not quite grief but closer to terror, she knows her mother is dead before Matthew gets off the phone.

She hears him say, "We'll call you right back," hears him pause, just a minute before coming back to the bedroom, watches him take both of her hands and then a deep breath.

"Something bad?" she says, shaking her head like a TV victim, her voice already the unfamiliar pleading of a mother-less child.

Later that day, Julie will learn that sometime in the night her mother woke her father up to ask him what it felt like when he was having a heart attack, and he described it to her in great detail, and she said, "That isn't like this," and he offered to take her to emergency, and she refused.

But now, sitting in her bed with her dogs on all sides of her and Matthew holding her hands Julie can only see her mother like a newscast from Somalia, cheeks sunken, eyes hollow, three fingers extended from one bony hand.

Julie's mother was supposed to go to the dentist that morning, and her father tried to wake her up several times, with several minutes in between—minutes in which the panic must have slowly mounted, realization seeping over him like an icy dark wave.

On the phone he says, "I keep asking the paramedics why they can't bring one of those machines in here," his voice losing itself in sobs. "I keep saying, why can't they do like they do on TV?"

"She didn't have any pain," Julie tells him. "And she didn't have any fear."

"And now they want to take her away," he says. "Should I let them take her away?"

"I'll be there as soon as I can get on a plane," Julie tells him. "Hang in there."

"There's a lady here who wants to talk to you, from the funeral home. I can't seem to answer any questions."

There is a loud shuffling and someone whose voice Julie has never heard before tells her utterly without emotion how sorry she is for her loss.

"It was your mother's wish to be cremated," the voice begins, "but we are having a little trouble engaging reality here, you know what I mean?"

"We?" Julie says.

"Your father can't decide whether to hold up on the cremation till you've had a chance to see the body. To tell you the truth, I don't think he's prepared for the fact of cremation at all."

"Prepared?" Julie says.

"What it boils down to, you see, is a question of finances."

Julie fixes her eyes on Matthew, bare-chested, who has started the lawn mower and who is now pushing it in ever diminishing squares around the big garden in the center of the yard.

"If we don't cremate today, we'll have to embalm, which of course will wind up being a wasted embalming upon cremation."

Julie counts the baby corn stalks that have come up already: twenty-seven from forty seeds, a good ratio.

"On the other hand, you only have one chance to make

the right decision. So if you are willing to handle the expense of embalming, well, it's your funeral."

"I don't think she would have wanted anyone to see her, even me," Julie says, maybe to herself, maybe out loud. She wants only to get back in bed beside Matthew, pull the dogs on top of her and replan her day in the garden. She thinks about the radishes ready to be eaten for dinner and the spinach that will bolt if she doesn't pick it in a few days.

"In this heat though," the voice continues, "time is of the essence, the body has already begun to change color, and if we don't embalm today, it will be a real mess by tomorrow."

"Does she look especially thin to you?" Julie says, before she can stop herself.

"Well, like I say," the voice picks up, ignoring her, "rate of putrefaction in the summer is triple that in all the other seasons."

I cannot leave, Julie thinks suddenly, without planting the rest of the tomatoes.

"Go ahead and cremate her," Julie says. "I can't be there until tomorrow."

"They're going to take her away," Julie tells her father. "It's going to be okay though. We have to do what she wanted."

"Are you coming?"

"Yes," she says. "Soon. I love you," she says, trying the words out on her father for the first time since she was five.

There is a muffled choking, and then the line goes dead. Julie hangs up the phone and walks out in the middle of the yard to Matthew. She says, "I think I am about to become valuable to my father."

After a lifetime of nervous visits to her parents' house, Julie walks into what is, she reminds herself, now only her father's house, as nervous as she has ever been. She can hear Strauss, the "Emperor Waltz," or is it "Delirium," make its way from her father's study to the kitchen door.

The cat waddles up to her, yelling for food. No one ever comes to the house without bringing a treat for the cat.

"I thought cats were supposed to run away when somebody dies," Julie says, to no one.

"Run?" Matthew would say, if he were here. "That?"

Julie's father emerges from his study looking more bewildered than anything else. They embrace the way people do who wear reading glasses around their necks, stiff and without really pressing.

"Look at all these things," Julie's father says when they separate, sweeping his hand around the living room, "all these things she did." And he is right, Julie's mother is in the room without being there, her perfectly handmade flowered slip covers, her airy taste in art, her giant, temperamental ferns.

"I told the minister you would speak at the service," Julie's father says. "She would have wanted that. She would have wanted you to say something nice about her. She said you never did in real life."

"That will be easy," Julie says.

"Of course it will," he says quietly. "She was the most wonderful woman in the world." He starts to sob again, lifetime-sized tears falling onto the cat who sits, patient as a Buddha, at his feet.

That night before the funeral, Julie dreams that she is sitting with her mother and father in the living room. Her mother is wearing Julie's favorite dress, one that she has given away years before. The furniture is the more comfortable, older style of her childhood, her favorite toys are strewn around the room. It is as though everything in the dream has been arranged to make her feel secure. A basket full of garden vegetables adorns the table, untouched.

"I thought you were dead," Julie says to her mother.

"I am," her mother says, crossing her ankles and folding her hands in her lap. "But I'll stay around until you can stand to be without me, until I know the two of you are going to be all right." She smoothes the hair around her face and smiles. "Then I'll just fade away."

It is the first in a series of dreams that will be with Julie for years, her mother dissolving before her eyes, until she becomes as thin as a piece of paper, until Julie cries out, often waking Matthew, "No, I'm not ready yet," and her mother solidifies, right before her eyes.

On the morning of the funeral, all Julie can think of is to cook, so she goes to the market across the street for bacon and eggs and buttermilk biscuits, and comes back and does the dishes that have already begun to accumulate.

"If you put the glasses in the dishwasher right side up, I discovered, they get all full of water," her father says.

Julie excuses herself, shuts the bathroom door behind her, and bursts into tears.

Julie fries bacon and eggs and bakes biscuits and stirs gravy as if her life depends on it. Her father gives at least half of his breakfast to the cat who is now apparently allowed to lie right on top of the dining room table with her head on the edge of his plate.

They talk about the changes that will come to his life, about him getting a microwave, about a maid coming in once a week. They talk about Julie coming east for his birthday next month, about him coming west for the winter. They talk about the last trip the three of them took together to Florida. Did Julie remember that it had rained, like magic, only in the evenings, did she remember how they had done the crossword puzzle, the three of them all together? And even though Julie doesn't remember, she tells him that she does. They talk about Julie's mother, words coming out of her father's mouth that make her believe in heaven, she's so desperate for her mother to hear. Finally, and only after they have talked about everything else, Julie and her father talk about sports.

Before the funeral is something the minister calls the interment of the ashes. Julie and her father both have their own vision of what this word means. Julie's involves a hand thrown pot sitting next to a fountain, her father, still stuck on the burial idea, imagines a big marble tomb, opened for the service and cemented back up.

What actually happens is that the minister digs up a three-inch square of ivy in an inconspicuous corner of the garden, digs a couple of inches of dirt beneath it, and sprinkles what amounts to little more than a heaping tablespoon of ashes into the hole.

Julie can feel her father leaning over her shoulder as she too leans over to see into the hole, whatever laws of physics she knows not being able to prepare her for the minusculity of those ashes, a whole human being so light that she could be lifted and caught by the wind.

The sun breaks through the clouds then, and the minister smiles, in cahoots with his god's timing, and takes that opportunity to refill the hole with dirt, and neatly replaces the ivy.

Later, inside the parish house, Julie's father says to the minister, "So there's really no limit to the number of people who could be cremated and inter . . . ned," his voice falling around the word, "into that garden."

"Oh, I guess upwards of sixty-eight thousand," the minister answers with a smile that Julie cannot read.

Her father has that bewildered look on his face again, the look of a man who never expected to have to feel sorry for all the things he didn't say. She pulls gently on his hand and he lets her, and they walk hand in hand to the car.

After the reception, after all the well-wishers have gone home, Julie's father turns on the Strauss again, this time "Tales From the Vienna Woods."

People have brought food, so much of it, Julie thinks it is like they are trying to make some kind of a point, and she sorts through it mechanically, what to refrigerate, what to freeze.

It has begun raining, huge hard summer raindrops, soaking the ground and turning her mother, Julie realizes almost happily, back to the earth, to ivy food, to dust.

She watches her father amble around the living room, directionless for a while, watches a smile cross his lips, perhaps for the rain, and then fade.

"Listen to this sequence," he tells her. "Is it possible that the music gets better than this in heaven?"

Something buzzes in Julie's chest now every time her father speaks to her in this new way, a little blast of energy that lightens her somehow, that buoys her up. It is a sensation, she realizes, with only a touch of alarm, not unlike falling in love.

"She would have loved to have heard the things you said about her," her father says.

"Yeah," Julie says, "she would have loved to hear what you said, too."

"Maybe she did," he says, "from . . . somewhere."

"Maybe," Julie says.

"We always get it wrong, this family . . . ," he says, and Julie waits for him to finish, but he gets lost, all of a sudden as the record changes to the "Acceleration Waltz."

"I love you so much," her father says, suddenly, and Julie turns, surprised, to face him.

But it is the cat he has lifted high and heavy above his head, and he and the cat begin turning together to the tryptic throb of the music. He holds the cat's left paw in one hand, supporting her weight, all the fluffy rolls of her, with the other, nuzzling her coffee-stained nose to the beat of the music until she makes a gurgling noise in her throat and threatens to spit. He pulls his head away from her and continues to spin, faster and faster, the music gaining force, their circles getting bigger around Julie's mother's flowered furniture, underneath Julie's mother's brittle ferns.

"One two three, one two three, one two three," Julie's father says, as the waltz reaches its full crescendo, and the cat seems to relax a little at the sound of his voice, and now she throws her head back into the spinning, as if agreeing to accept the weight of this new love that will from this day forward be thrust upon her.

# CONTRIBUTORS

SHEN CHRISTENSON lives in two Utah towns—Salt Lake City and Boulder—with her four children and partner, A. J. Martine. She is pursuing an M.F.A. in creative writing at the University of Utah. Her story, "Facts," won *Story* magazine's short story competition in 1993. Her fiction has also been published in *The Quarterly, Alaska Quarterly Review, Hayden's Ferry Review,* and *Denver Quarterly.* "Mouth to Mouth" appeared in *Other Voices.*

Shen writes:

> Writer and mentor François Camoin is fond of saying: "Beware the fiction that makes you pound your breast and exclaim 'How True! How True! And How Well Said!'" He warns that the best fiction never panders to the notion that we can see the world clearly and that language can explain it.
>
> So I thought "Mouth to Mouth" would be easy to write. I'd begin with a real event that even the newspapers were quick to describe as "unimaginable," "unspeakable," and "inhuman." And

I gave my narrator the nagging memory of this event's central image, children's bodies on the sidewalk. How better to dramatize how unexplainable the world really is? It didn't work. "Mouth to Mouth," instead, opened up a new problem for me—the world of those things we seem eager to pretend we *don't* understand, *can't* understand, when in fact we do. This was a story that seemed to twist itself at every turn and to insist on showing the underbelly of mother love. The story let me start with a mother throwing children off a balcony to their deaths, and then, for the rest of the ride, it refused to let me pretend I couldn't see a human reason behind that.

KATHARINE COLES's second collection of poems, *The Walk-Through Heart*, will be published in 1995. Her poetry and fiction have appeared in *The Paris Review*, *Poetry*, *The New Republic* and *North American Review*, among other magazines. She has received an Individual Writer's Fellowship and a New Forms Project Grant from the National Endowment for the Arts, as well as the 1994 Mayor's Award for the Arts. Coles is a professor of English at Westminster College in Salt Lake City, where she teaches creative writing and directs the Westminster Poetry Series.

Katharine writes:

"Why I Left Paradise" began on a Saturday morning in March 1989. The night before, I had given a reading at A Book Store in Logan, Utah, with Utah poet G. Barnes, and afterwards a group of writers stayed up late, playing the guitar and singing in a room at the Baugh Motel, which has a trout stream in the backyard and pictures of sheep printed on the towels. One woman in our group, Linda Rawlins, sang "Old Paint" and broke our hearts. The next morning, we had breakfast at the old Black Jack Cafe, which was in what I remember (inaccurately) as a dirt-floored lean-to hanging off the back of a country store located in the north section of the Logan Valley. The Black Jack is gone now, but in 1989 it served eggs and potatoes with just the right amount of grease to make you want to go back to bed. We were driving back south toward Logan on a country road through sheep ranches when poet Chip Rawlins told a great yarn about pyromania and why they almost got gun control in a small town where he'd lived. While he was talking, I started to hear a voice—Dawna's—giving her version, a sort of sub-text, the true inside story. She said, "It all started the first time Dimmer burned down Harris's trailer," and she kept going from there.

To say I stole the story isn't quite right. First of all, Chip Rawlins willingly lent it to me, knowing full well he wouldn't recognize it when it came back. Second, Dawna is an entirely invented character, as are the others. Last, his story was about small-town politics, and Dawna's story is definitely about sex. The incendiary kind.


PAM HOUSTON is a river and hunting guide, but not a hunter. She has taught creative writing at her alma mater, Denison University, and is a Ph.D. candidate at the University of Utah. She has published nonfiction and fiction in magazines ranging from *Mirabella* to *Mademoiselle*, as well as in literary magazines such as *Cimarron Review*, *Crazyhorse*, and *The Gettysburg Review*. Her collection of stories, *Cowboys Are My Weakness*, was published by W.W. Norton, and released in paperback by Washington Square Press. She is writing a novel and editing an anthology on women and hunting.

Pam writes:

> I've always suspected good things about my father because he and I share similar sensibilities. "Waltzing the Cat" came from the scene where my father lifted our cat on the day of my mother's funeral. In that moment I saw him clearly. Some of the story is invented, of course. There was no music, for instance, and while it's true that I never heard my father say "I love you," I never thought for a minute that when he said that he was talking to me. One thing that makes this story unique is that it's the only story I've written in third-person. The other thing that was unusual was to be at the funeral of my mother, whom I loved deeply. I was there and I was mourning, but I was also aware of myself as a writer, taking notes in my head. I was thinking: "Why is this fiction happening in front of me?"

SHELLEY HUNT was born in El Paso, Texas. In 1979, she migrated to Salt Lake City to experience winter. She has worked as a silversmith, waitress, vocalist, housekeeper, and file clerk. She is currently mothering a half-dozen or so boys and is an M.F.A. student in creative writing at the University of Utah. She has published in *Utah Holiday* and in the second edition of *What If? Exercises for Fiction Writers.*

Shelley writes:

> The birth process has always been, for me, cathartic; the supreme marathon. When I discovered in 1989 that I was pregnant, I was both terrified and ecstatic. Finally it was my turn. I had coached births in the past, so I knew what I was in for and this both helped and hindered.
>
> A friend told me that all women become acquainted with death in childbirth. I think it was that dichotomy that compelled me to crave something so violent as to want to split myself in half. (During labor, my friend, Jacqueline, kept announcing to the son in her belly: "You are really pissing me off.") "Where Detail in the Background is Permissible" comes out of those years when I craved birth but did not think I would ever experience it, and from the terror I felt when I knew I would. I found the title in an old photographic manual, captioning a photo of a young boy, a dog, and a painting.

HELEN WALKER JONES has published fiction in *Harper's, Indiana Review, Chariton Review, Apalachee Quarterly, Florida Review,* and *Gargoyle,* among others. As a technical writer, she recently finished a script for an infomercial. She lives in Salt Lake City with her husband, Walter, and their two children.

Helen writes:

> The image that triggered the writing of this story was a beat-up

sedan loaded with six broad-shouldered, pony-tailed men in cowboy hats. When I saw this vehicle cruising Fifth East in Salt Lake, it reminded me of my childhood, growing up in Southern Alberta forty miles from the Blood Indian Reserve. During harvest, many Indians came to work in the sugarbeet fields, and they were a constant presence in my hometown during the summer. Also, in college I had a roommate who was a member of Alaska's Tlingit tribe, and I was fascinated by her stories of Indian life and culture. I had her caustic sense of humor in mind when I created the character of Veronica Waxwing.

PATRICIA McCONNEL is the author of two books, including *Sing Soft, Sing Loud*, a book of fiction published by Atheneum in 1989. She is the winner of two creative writing fellowships from the National Endowment for the Arts, wrote one of the Ten Best PEN Short Stories of 1984, and read at the Library of Congress in 1985. She has published short stories and articles, and is working on a novel about a woman traveling alone, on foot, in the desert of southeastern Utah in the mid-1930s. She lives in Blanding, Utah, when she is not in the canyon outback in her truck, Serafina. McConnel has equipped Serafina with a teapot, a CD player, and a laptop computer, and calls herself a "high-tech hunter-gatherer."

Patricia writes:

"The Way I Live" was the result of several disparate elements in my life coming together randomly, their only relationship being concurrence in time. I had returned to Utah after spending two years in Las Vegas, where I was depressed at what I saw going on and even more depressed because no one but me seemed to be bothered by it. Once back in Utah, I lived in a trailer in a campground, both of which I have accurately recreated in the story in every detail, including busted pipes and no sewage. I remember lying on my bunk one day when the pump that supplied our well water had quit again, thinking that if my mother were still alive she'd have a hard time understanding the way I choose to live my life. That thought eventually became the first line of the story, but I didn't recognize it as such at the time.

Not long after that I read "The Suburbs of Eden" by Katharine Coles, a story in which the main character is worrying about the risks her mother takes in her career as an archaeologist. It was Katie's story that finally triggered "The Way I Live," perhaps because I knew Katie's real-life mother, although not an archaeologist, used to be a geologist and is a mountain climber, and it amused me that Katie and I both get a lot of literary mileage out of our mothers. I say "perhaps" because these things happen in hidden recesses of the creative mind and I am never sure about them.

The best part, though, is that after Katie read the story, she called me to say, "Do you know that my mother's name is Miriam?"

I said, "I thought her name is Joan."

"It is, but it used to be Miriam. And you don't know, either, that my grandmother's name is Miriam too?"

"You have never referred to her as anything but Grandmamá."

So there you have it. Coincidence might explain why I chose a name for my character that is also the name of Katie's mother. It becomes less likely that just by coincidence my friend's mother, like the Miriam in the story, changed her given name, but the odds are astronomical against coincidence explaining that Katie's mother and grandmother are both Miriams and that Miriam "Jr." changed her name.

Clearly there was an intense psychic connection between me and Katie during this period. Skeptics will say that Katie must have told me these things at one time and I forgot I knew them, but Katie and I know better. Anyway, for the reasons above I dedicate the story to Katie Coles, and call it her story. It is great fun to have it finally appear in a collection with a story of hers.

PAULINE MORTENSEN is the author of a collection of short stories, *Back Before the World Turned Nasty*, published by the University of Arkansas Press in 1989. Although she has published in various literary magazines across the country, she is currently in exile from academia and writes for money and pleasure in Orem, Utah.

Pauline writes:

To write a story like "Blue, Blue, My Love Is Blue," it helps if you have a few dozen crazy relatives, relatives who have a lot of creative ways of messing up their own lives and everybody else's. It also helps if none of them can read. I am very lucky in this way, poised between the heart of darkness and the light at the end of the tunnel.

I came to write this story because out of all the crazy voices talking in my head, this one was screaming the loudest. Out of all the chaos that was this woman's life, there was so little that could be done, just too much to puzzle over and not enough to understand. I found I could write this story for her. And for me, strike that delicate balance between the chaos and articulation.

DIANNE NELSON's collection of short stories, *A Brief History of Male Nudes in America*, won the 1993 Flannery O'Connor Award for short fiction and was published by the University of Georgia Press. She has won two Utah Arts Council writing awards and an Associated Writing Program Intro Award. Her short fiction has been published in *The Quarterly*, *The New England Review*, *The Iowa Review*, and *Ploughshares*, among others. She earned an M.F.A. in creative writing from Arizona State University.

Dianne writes:

"In the Shadows of Upshot-Knothole" was the last story I wrote for my collection, *A Brief History of Male Nudes in America*, and I purposely wanted it to be different from the earlier pieces I had written. I decided to go back into territory I had never written about—my own infancy on the southwestern Utah ranch where I was born. The backdrop of the 1950s atomic testing seemed to be just the right strange and quietly malevolent edge I wanted to give this story. My real handle into the narrative came when I decided to have myself as an almost omniscient baby tell parts of this story. The dressed-up pigs, the soldiers in trenches, my wannabe movie star father—all pieces of the truth that finally found a home together.

LYNNE BUTLER OAKS lives in Salt Lake City with her husband and three children. "Sisterwives: The Order Things Took" was first published by Hometown Press. It received the Ruth Hindman Foundation's H. E. Francis Fiction Prize and was nominated for a 1993 Pushcart Prize. She has published stories in *Fiction International*, *StoryQuarterly*, *The Quarterly*, *The Missouri Review*, and *Utah Holiday*.

Lynne writes:

I spent my teen years chemically clean, so to speak. It was really no great feat in Utah, even in the 1960s. Not so with religion, though. I inhaled. Any good Marxist could have spotted me. So, if we're locating things, this story flashes back to then and there. To 1969. I made my first attempts at the writing of it in 1989, shortly after the too-young death of a woman who somehow manages to appear alongside every memory I have of being young. That she was too is probably all she would want me to say about her.

About the story: I confess I have no idea if there are polygamists living anywhere near Bear Lake, the lake on the northern borders of Utah and Idaho. There are raspberry fields there, though. And there were raspberry fields for us when we were young. They were real enough, and like everything else around us then, figured heavily into the truth.

MARCELYN RITCHIE, an avid NBA basketball fan, is an M.F.A. candidate in creative writing at the University of Utah. She drives west from Salt Lake City every chance she gets.

Marcelyn writes:

"Nevada Border Towns" started as a story about my grandmother's filing system. The summer after my freshman year in college I lived with my grandparents in Oakland, California. Each night over dinner we would debate various topics. One evening my grandmother asked me to help her locate an article to support her argument. I pulled open her filing drawer. She had files from "Adversity to Zion," she said proudly. They sounded like the names of horses to me.

NICOLE STANSBURY teaches creative writing at Salt Lake Community College. Her novel, *The Lucy Stories*, won the Utah Arts Council's publication prize in 1989. She has published stories in *ThreePenny Review*, *Yellow Silk* and *Prism International*. She earned an M.F.A. degree in creative writing at the University of Utah.

Nicole writes:

This story, "Some Body Parts Remember a War," happened out of love and sorrow. And also out of a few gorgeous lines of poetry, penned by a friend and fellow writer, Richelle Hawks: "Just seeing myself in her, I stop bleeding/ and there was no one there to speak highly of me." The story, of course, is for k. d. lang.

JAN STUCKI is pursuing a Ph.D. in creative writing at the

University of Utah. She has published fiction in *StoryQuarterly* and *Sun Dog*. Her work won *Willow Springs*'s 1993 fiction prize, and first place in the 1994 Utah Arts Festival Short-Short Story Competition.

Jan writes:

A couple of years ago, on an island in the South Pacific, somebody found the sole of a shoe that they figured belonged to Amelia Earhart because it was her size—9N. Magazines published articles speculating on what fabulous international schemes she could have been tangled up in, but what got my attention—and it really did distract me—was that Amelia Earhart wore the same size shoe I wear.

A lot of women wear size 9N. Most of them, though, could forget this like an adult. But I had to parade around my Amelia Earhart feet like a five-year-old. I started to write about overgrown tropical islands with bits of metal and shoe on them. As I wrote, I realized that what really interested me was not the shoe, but the need for connection, the will to have something in common with someone who could not be more different from me, and the moments of isolation when that will is the strongest.